A STUDENT OF LIVING THINGS

FICTION BY SUSAN SHREVE

A Fortunate Madness

A Woman Like That

Children of Power

Miracle Play

Dreaming of Heroes

Queen of Hearts

A Country of Strangers

Daughters of the New World

The Visiting Physician

The Train Home

Plum & Jaggers

A STUDENT OF LIVING THINGS

SUSAN RICHARDS SHREVE

VIKING

VIKING
Published by the Penguin Group
Penguin Group (USA) Inc., 375 Hudson Street, New York, New York 10014, U.S.A.
Penguin Group (Canada), 90 Eglinton Avenue East, Suite 700, Toronto, Ontario,
Canada M4P 2Y3 (a division of Pearson Penguin Canada Inc.)
Penguin Books Ltd, 80 Strand, London WC2R 0RL, England
Penguin Ireland, 25 St. Stephen's Green, Dublin 2, Ireland
(a division of Penguin Books Ltd)
Penguin Books Australia Ltd, 250 Camberwell Road, Camberwell, Victoria 3124,
Australia (a division of Pearson Australia Group Pty Ltd)
Penguin Books India Pvt Ltd, 11 Community Centre, Panchsheel Park,
New Delhi – 110 017, India
Penguin Group (NZ), Cnr Airborne and Rosedale Roads, Albany, Auckland 1310,
New Zealand (a division of Pearson New Zealand Ltd)
Penguin Books (South Africa) (Pty) Ltd, 24 Sturdee Avenue, Rosebank,
Johannesburg 2196, South Africa

Penguin Books Ltd, Registered Offices: 80 Strand, London WC2R 0RL, England

First published in 2006 by Viking Penguin, a member of Penguin Group (USA) Inc.

10 9 8 7 6 5 4 3 2 1

ISBN 0-670-03758-3

Printed in the United States of America
Set in Berkeley Oldstyle Book with Polytone Global
Designed by Daniel Lagin

Too small, no more

For

Theo and Noah, new treasures

and

Russell and Bich and Jessica

ACKNOWLEDGMENTS

I would like to thank my editors Carole DeSanti and Hilary Redmon and all the team at Viking and especially thanks to my agent Gail Hochman for her tireless work and commitment and straightforward good sense. Thanks to my long-suffering in-house reader Timothy Seldes and to Porter Shreve and Howard Norman for their excellent advice on this book.

I am lucky to know and love the gifted composer and pianist Timothy Andres, who provided the musical scores for this book.

My daughter Kate introduced me to her love of science, which provided the central metaphor for *A Student of Living Things* and brought me into the far outer circle of that exciting and mysterious world. She and Rosanna Bruno are responsible for Claire's artwork in "The Lifeguard Chair" sections.

Thanks finally and always to my family—Po, Bich, Eq, Rusty, Caleb, Jess, Kate and Timothy, my agent for life.

CONTENTS

I. AUGUST II: THE MORNING
OF MY BROTHER'S BIRTHDAY   1
The Lifeguard Chair   13

II. APRIL 4: MINOR IMPERFECTIONS   15
The Lifeguard Chair   63

III. APRIL 5: MUTATIONS   65
The Lifeguard Chair   75

IV. MAY 3: INCOMPLETE METAMORPHOSIS   77
The Lifeguard Chair   115

V. THE EVOLUTION OF SOHPIA LUPE   117
The Lifeguard Chair   143

VI. ADAPTATION   145
The Lifeguard Chair   177

VII. SYMBIOSIS   179
The Lifeguard Chair   199

VIII. BENJAMIN IN THE FLESH   201

IX. THE AFTERNOON OF OCTOBER 22   223

I.

AUGUST 11: THE MORNING OF MY BROTHER'S BIRTHDAY

Today is my brother's twenty-seventh birthday. It's only seven in the morning, one of those hot, brown, swampy days in Washington, the air so thick it's difficult to breathe. Children drape like damp cloths over the fire hydrants, around the lampposts, too weary to play. The long-suffering National Guardsmen, half asleep in their fatigues and sidearms, lean against the cool marble of government buildings.

I've arrived early at the Eastern Market, since my mother will be coming for a special lunch this afternoon—the first time she has been to my apartment since I moved away from home. She'll bring her sister, my aunt Faith, and perhaps her son, my cousin, who lost his leg four years ago in an explosion.

"His leg but not his life," my mother says every time his name, which is Bernard, comes up.

My mother would prefer to recognize the day of my brother's murder. It's in her character, just as it's in my father's to celebrate the day of Steven's birth, to slip over the evening of April 4, when my only brother was shot on the steps of the George Washington University Gelman Library, where he was studying for his law exams. My father likes to think the years will continue to accumulate to Steven, although our memory of him is locked in at twenty-five. I understand the feelings of both of my parents and neither of them. It's the way with parents—just as you think you know them, they slide away like mercury breaking into slippery bits that would take endless patience to reassemble.

I am no longer a patient woman.

The market is southeast of the Capitol, near Union Station, and is open every morning from 6:00 A.M. until 2:00, although recently the vendors have been closing down quickly at noon, loading their trucks and beating it out of town during the lunch hour, when trouble, if it's going to happen, usually begins.

This morning I wander through the stalls, pleased to be in the company of people, pressing against women who lean over the wooden tables with their fruits and vegetables to weigh. We smile back and forth, familiar to one another, since most of us shop every day, buying little, only sufficient to last through breakfast the next morning, a sense of transience about our lives.

For months before Steven was killed, there had been a silent civil war, fear creeping under the skin, a menacing suspicion of one group of people for another, a distrust of the outsider in a city of outsiders.

Now we've been in a state of emergency for almost three weeks— the National Guard circling the city of Washington—something that has happened only once in recent memory, during the riots that broke out after the death of Martin Luther King, Jr. Now there seems to be an actual civil war, difficult to describe.

"Who to trust?" my mother asked at a recent Sunday dinner, turning the front page of the newspaper facedown. "It's as if everyone is the enemy or could be."

"This country isn't a safe house, Julia," my father said.

"Then I want to move," she said, getting up from the table, clearing the plates, turning on the water to rinse them.

"Where would we go?" I asked.

"Away!" she said with conviction, as if she knew a route.

"Try these." A withered, prune-faced woman, burned dark by the sun, gives me a taste of artichokes mixed with chickpeas and spices. It's delicious.

I love these small Jerusalem artichokes and think I'll make a salad of them for lunch with sweet tomatoes and maybe mango, which is ripe and not too soft, even in this heat. The goat cheese is light, and I get a small piece of it rolled in herbs and crusty olive bread and roasted red peppers, which the vendor says she makes herself.

I think a lot about food, especially sweets and fruit, the rosy fruits in particular. Peaches and plums and cherries.

Every morning since Asa was three weeks old—and he's almost three months now—I walk from my apartment along East Capitol past Lincoln Park to the market, and, walking, I babble to Asa and think about food. I buy, of course, but very little. I don't eat that much myself, skinny with nerves, and Asa is still nursing. But I imagine putting meals together, elaborate meals to which I'd invite strangers who would become friends, women with children and single men and fathers and soldiers, some of the people I see day after day at the market. We speak, but I don't know their names.

"I'm having a lunch party," I say to the woman vendor who gave me the artichoke dip to taste.

"Very nice!" She pops a raspberry into my mouth. "Good?"

"Excellent," I say.

"Who's coming to your luncheon?" she asks.

"My mother. Do you know her?"

"Your mother?"

"She's small with curly hair, which hasn't gone gray yet."

I'm proud of that about my mother. Her hair, still dark at almost sixty, gives me a sense of permanence.

"I know your mother, of course," the woman says. "She comes with you on weekends, all the way in town from the suburbs."

"Her name is Mrs. Frayn," I say, to place her as a friend.

People in Washington know about our family because of Steven. Not that it's unusual for a young man to die here. Many have been killed in the twenty years since we moved from New York City, when Steven was seven and I was three. But then the violence was personal, drugs or guns or gang warfare or domestic quarrels, and in the last few months it's a random bomb or arson or a staged accident, and several are injured or die at once.

Steven was assassinated in the late afternoon, and he was alone, except I was standing beside him. It wasn't an accident that he was the one chosen.

"It'll be my mother's first visit to my apartment," I say to the woman vendor for no particular reason, except I feel I owe her something personal about myself since she gave me a raspberry. I'm careful about these things, avoiding obligations, wishing to keep a balance with people even in matters as small as this.

"Your father's coming to lunch, too?"

I shake my head, a reserve settling over me. It isn't her business about my father's plans, but I answer anyway, which I know isn't necessary, but I have that need to respond to any question.

"Learn to say shut up," my mother says to me. "Two words. Very simple."

But I never do.

"My father's working," I say, although it isn't exactly true.

My father's a professor of medicine at George Washington University, where Steven and I went to school and graduate school. He's on summer holiday from classes, but today he's probably in his hangar rebuilding an airplane that has taken up most of our backyard since I can remember and much of my father's time, especially since Steven's death. It's an old World War II fighter plane that he bought at an auction, and he's in the long process of restoring it to its original shape.

But he wouldn't come to lunch at my apartment in any case.

Our house is in the suburbs just over the northern city line, where the land flattens, spreading into the horizon now dotted with high-rises and strip malls and corporate headquarters. Before there were houses, our suburb was a flatland forest, slightly higher than the swamp city of Washington, with scrubby trees and low brush, a kind of primordial look about the land, as if nature had had its way with it once and could again.

Ours was the last of the old suburbs to be built, because the land to the north is the least hospitable, so the houses are more temporary in structure than other suburban houses, put up quickly to accommodate scientists like my father who come from all over the world to work in laboratories at the National Institutes of Health. We have a one-story rectangular house, with the hangar taking up much of the garden, which wouldn't be a sufficient garden anyway, the soil too sandy, water at a premium, especially in the summer months. In the summer my mother takes a white plastic chair with a cushion out to the garden, puts it down beside the hangar, and reads her newspapers.

There's a study and three bedrooms: one for my mother and father, one that was Steven's, one belonging to my father's brother, Milo, who's a concert pianist down on his luck. When Milo moved in, my father built a little house to the side of our house but attached to it, opening from the kitchen. That was my room from the time I was twelve years old.

"You must understand that I can't come visit you in your apartment, Claire," my father said to me when I was packing up to move. "*You* should be living in *my* home."

I did understand. Perhaps he was more upset than he knew that I was having a baby out of wedlock, because we're an old-fashioned family, although not religious, holding to the daily rituals of an orderly life, and for good reason.

But I know it isn't the baby—he's glad to have this baby, although he's never asked who the father is and would be distraught to know and doesn't in general believe it's a good thing to bring a baby into a troubled time. But it is *life,* and he knows that or he wouldn't be rebuilding an airplane, hoping that once it's completed he'll be able to fly it. Of course, he doesn't consider *how* he'll fly or where he'll be permitted to take off and land or what rules of the air would apply to a novice with a rebuilt warplane. And that's the point. One doesn't think of these things, or babies would never be born in wartime.

My moving was a failure to him. I think he was embarrassed that his family couldn't hold together under one roof after Steven died. He thought it was a reflection of his weakness. But he's not a weak man, and he misses me and wishes I were there every morning at breakfast, both for his pride and my company. Milo can be sullen, and my mother is argumentative, and I am sunlight to him, though God knows not so bright as the days we've been having this summer.

My father isn't the one who asked me to call the baby Steven. My mother did. But, typically, she said it was at my father's request and he didn't want to impose; nevertheless it would mean a great deal to him, and after all, what immortality is there for the dead unless the living hold on to their names?

I suppose I believe that, too. If I believe in any immortality, it would have to be the passing on of names of the dead to the babies, as the Jews do.

I thought about Steven as a name and couldn't live with it. I'm superstitious by nature, and to give a baby my brother's name seemed as if I were asking bad luck for Asa. Besides, and this perhaps is the more important: I loved Steven.

I should clarify the irony of our situation. We aren't Jewish or Muslim, and Christian only to the degree that until the 9/11 attack on the United States, when we began living with this whispering civil unrest, we were halfhearted Quakers, believing in what my father calls "peaceful coexistence."

My mother, born Jewish, has never been a natural believer of any kind, but my father is still a member of the Society of Friends.

"In principle," he says. "But in practice it's foolish to stand in a war zone and turn the other cheek."

I am a biologist.

When my mother used to introduce me to people at the glass-blowing factory where she's a designer, she'd say with real emotion in her voice, "My daughter, Claire, is a student of living things."

Since Steven's death her voice assumes a flat and hollow tone.

"My daughter, Claire, is a student of living things. Hah!"

And the "Hah!" has the rattle of a final breath.

"A true believer," Steven used to say of me when we went to the university together. It amused him, my love for what he called the "creepy crawlies" and "fuzzy wuzzies" and "slippy slimies" that decorated my bedroom.

But true belief is fairy dust, and I'm a scientist.

———————

It's after eight, and I've finished marketing. Asa is fussing because he's ready to nurse, and I'm looking for my friend Eva, who's been my dearest friend since fourth grade. It's Wednesday, and we've arranged as usual to meet at the market before she goes to work. If there weren't this civil upheaval, Eva would be a dancer, but, as it is, she's a technician at the hospital where Steven was taken when he was shot. So she was the one who called my parents to say there'd been a catastrophe.

We used to do everything together, but after my brother was killed, her parents wouldn't permit her to go to public places with me—not even a film or a restaurant, certainly not the busy market.

I'm a marked woman. It's difficult to be my friend.

Nevertheless, every day or two we try to meet at the market to catch up. She doesn't tell her parents, of course, and isn't as concerned about being in my company as they are for her.

"But I have to tell you, Claire. I do worry," she has said on occasion.

I look around, staying longer than I had planned, but Eva doesn't seem to be here, and just her absence this particular day, perhaps because it's Steven's birthday, is a bad omen to me.

"No meat for your lunch?" the vendor asks, holding up a chicken roasted on a spit and smothered in herbs.

I shake my head.

"Vegetarian?" she asks.

"It's too hot for meat," I say.

The vendor has come around the corner of her kiosk and is leaning over Asa, reaching under the umbrella I've attached to his stroller to protect him.

"Fat," she says, looking at him and shaking her head. "He's eating you up."

Something about her interest alarms me, so I say, "Thank you" and "That will be all for today," and I dip the umbrella so Asa is no longer visible to the assembled shoppers.

As I lift my head from covering Asa, brush my hair off my forehead, my eyes readjusting to the brightness, I see someone familiar at the next kiosk, and my heart drops.

He's standing with his back to me, a rolled bandanna around his head, his hair longer than the last time I saw him, curling over the collar of his work shirt. He's purchasing artichokes and black olives and olive oil. Surprising for someone who's come here for a different purpose than marketing.

I know this man, although I haven't seen him since last August. And I know why he's here this morning, pretending to shop, actually buying things he doesn't need, reaching across another shopper for figs.

He's come here to watch me.

Victor Duarte—the name he gave me when I met him a month after Steven's death—is short and stocky, swarthy with tiny black bean eyes. I used to think he was handsome, with an earthy sexuality, a rough tenderness about him. But what did I know then?

He's watching me now. I feel his eyes as I hurry away from the market, not running but moving with dispatch, so I'll seem purposeful but not afraid. I don't turn around for some time, maybe two city blocks, and when I do, no one is behind me that I can see, except an old woman with her marketing in a cloth satchel struggling up the hill and an unpleasant-looking, short-haired brown dog who according to the laws of this city should be on a leash.

My apartment is about a mile from the market on a steady upward incline, so I'm breathless pushing the stroller when I arrive. From my living room on the seventh floor, I can see the city. It looks like the black-and-white polka-dot dress Grandma Frayn used to wear to sing in the Welsh church choir. White splashed irregularly on a black background. When I stand in the large window facing north, what I see is an occasional streak of white spreading across the landscape where a random bomb has exploded, taking down a small building like National Bank and Trust on Wisconsin Avenue in the upper northwest, a gas station in the southeast along the Potomac, a grammar school in Capitol Hill, sufficient damage to leave a blank that from a distance in this sunny city is white.

This has happened since Steven died a year ago last April.

"He was the striking match," Uncle Milo said at dinner one night last winter. "Since 9/11, people have been uneasy, and then a plane carrying a high-school baseball team on its way to spring practice in Florida falls for no known reason into the Potomac River, and fatal levels of mercury are discovered at Cardozo High School, and a law student is assassinated on the steps of a university library."

"Because he said what he believed," Julia said, taking every conversation about my brother as an offensive attack.

"Or for nothing," Milo said. "Who knows?"

"You're insane, Milo," my mother said.

"Insane" has become her favorite word.

I moved to Capitol Hill when I was six months pregnant because of Asa's father, who had lived here growing up. Asa's grandfather still lives in the same row house on Second Street NE, behind the Supreme Court, two blocks from the Capitol. I don't know him, but I know about him, and sometimes I walk by his house, which is yellow with lacy vines running up the front, and I imagine him opening the front door just as I walk by, and I say, "Hello. I'm Claire Frayn, and this baby is your grandson, Asa."

But I've never seen him on my walks, which are in the daytime, so I probably never will.

I live on Eleventh Street just after A, on the top floor of a small prewar apartment house. My mother thinks it's dangerous with threats of terrorism to live so close to the Capitol, but I like that the streets are full of people, walking and shopping and eating, mothers like me with strollers, young men in ties who work for the government, children walking their dogs. Not that it feels safer than the suburbs where I grew up, just busier and less lonely.

I don't remember *fear*—not as a physiological condition, like the flu—until the night that Steven died. Now I have a kind of low-grade fever of anxiety all the time. I start at loud noises or high-pitched ones, at a screeching of brakes or a door slamming. I sleep well, well enough, my bed as far away from the window as possible, Asa in a basket in the corner beside me so nothing can fall on him.

This civil war is what earthquakes must have seemed like centuries ago, before anything was understood about fault lines or tectonic plates. There'll be a blast—like a firecracker, maybe a pipe bomb—in the distance, a crash and then a rumble, the hissing wind of an inferno. But the occasions are haphazard, almost careless in their planning. Days go by with nothing, and then a day of trouble will follow.

By the time I reach the front door of my apartment, I'm panting from the heat and the running and probably from fright. Certainly fear is what I'm feeling as I pick up Asa, drop my groceries in the stroller and push the 7 button on the elevator.

I've come to a decision. It's been on my mind for days, but after I saw Victor Duarte and tore off up the hill, Asa crying with hunger, a decision came without my even thinking about it.

When the elevator opens on the seventh floor, I rush down the hall, open the door to my apartment and sink into the sofa, lifting my shirt for Asa.

It's as if, all along in these last months, I've been in the process of discovering that I have a choice.

_____

My father answers the phone at the first ring.

"I thought you'd be in the hangar," I say.

"Too hot," he replies.

"Are you coming for lunch?" I ask.

"You *know* the answer to that already, Claire," he says.

"But I'd like you to come," I say quietly.

I wait for his inevitable hesitation, knowing he can't say no to me and won't say yes, and when he starts to speak, I can almost hear him arranging his sentence in such a way that he can accomplish neither denying me nor coming to lunch.

"Why?" he asks, to my surprise.

"Because I want you to be here," I say. "There's something I need to tell you."

I hang up the phone and lean against the stove, imagining the conversation I'll have with my parents at lunch.

For a year this month, my life has been at risk, and I've told no one—not Eva, not Lisha, not my family. This morning when I saw Victor Duarte looking for me at the market, I knew that the story I've kept a secret for a year is endangering all of us. When my family comes today, I will tell them the truth.

I'll begin on the morning of April 4, sixteen months ago, the day that Steven died.

THE LIFEGUARD CHAIR

My father gave me a lifeguard chair for my eighth birthday, which he had purchased at an auction in Lewes, Delaware. On weekends he and my mother scoured auctions and secondhand stores for treasures, and the chair he bought must have been used by lifeguards at one of the mid-Atlantic beaches—Rehoboth or Bethany or Dewey Beach. Why it was for sale, I don't know. But I used to imagine that it had been used by a life-guard who had died rescuing a drowning child. A young, sturdy, handsome lifeguard, and the child he had rescued was me.

My father put the lifeguard chair in our garden next to the airplane hangar, and that's when I began to keep my notebooks of observations. I have fifteen of them, spiral notebooks with unlined paper filled with notes, each one marking a year in my life.

I would climb up to the seat of the chair, not quite as high as the roof of the hangar but high enough to see the lineup of backyards on either side of us and in daylight to see inside the kitchen windows of the look-alike houses on our block.

The first entry was made on July 13, the day I turned eight.

Side one

Side two

This is my eye. It's brown with yellow spots and a black circle in the middle. One side of my eye, which is in the back, sees inside to my brain, and the other side, which is in the front, sees outside to the world.

But in order to see the world clearly, I need to wear glasses.

C.F., age 8

II.

APRIL 4: MINOR IMPERFECTIONS

I

April 4, a Tuesday, and a cold rain had been falling steadily for days. Streams of mud poured off the banks of the Potomac, flooding the river between the glassblowing factory in Alexandria and our house in the suburb of Bethesda. My mother had to spend the night at work.

I got up before dawn, slipping into jeans and flip-flops and the yellow T-shirt I'd tossed on the floor the night before—the bedroom damp and dark, sheets of rain sliding down the south wall of glass that created a greenhouse for the mass of plants I kept. And in the microcosm of a zoo where I'd slept since I was a child, the living creatures were complaining of hunger. Field mice and a snow-white rat, a one-winged finch I rescued from the grounds of George Washington University, two thin-bodied milk snakes and a praying mantis. Not to mention the collection of dead creatures—the fetus of a kitten in formaldehyde, the skeleton of a spider monkey, a cobra head, the bones of birds, a pile of feathers in the shape of a fan.

Every surface in my bedroom was a display for my personal museum of natural history.

I fed the noisy animals quickly, checked my watch—not yet seven—and headed to the kitchen. I'd promised my mother I'd be at the factory early if I could get across the bridges.

Milo was in the kitchen drinking a cup of coffee, licking the powdered sugar off a doughnut.

"Blissfully quiet without Julia this morning." He toasted me with his coffee cup.

"A silent tomb, is how I see it," I said defending my mother, who had after all opened our house to what remained of a small family—including Milo and her sister Faith and my cousin Bernard—who had moved in with their various complications and complaints, using as an excuse the fear of growing unrest in Washington, D.C.

"At least we don't have to blacken the morning with Julia's report of the police blotter," Milo went on, unable to help himself, a natural-born complainer.

My mother was keeping a mental record of the incidents of violence that had occurred all over the city beginning with the evening three years ago at the 7-Eleven in Foggy Bottom when an explosion of a bomb handmade by an unemployed high-school dropout cost my cousin Bernard his right leg below the knee. The most recent incident was Sunday, the day before yesterday, when a young man in Lafayette Park, across the street from the White House, set himself on fire, injuring a policeman and burning, although not seriously, a cocker spaniel on a walk with his owner. Fourteen incidents within the ten square miles of this city since our family had become personally connected with what my father referred to as "the disintegration of order" in Washington, D.C. A civilized order was important to my father.

"Oh, Milo, don't be so difficult," I said, taking a doughnut for myself.

"Difficult, my foot! I'm a complicated artist with a fragile nervous system." He grabbed my hand and kissed it, one of his Viennese kisses, fashioning himself a large talent in the wrong city and the wrong century.

"So off you go, and think of me always on your journey."

Down the long, narrow hall of our meandering, one-story, carelessly constructed suburban tract house, where all the bedrooms were located except mine, and that because of the zoo smells that came from my room, my father was taking a shower. The rest of the house was silent.

I poured coffee into a traveling mug, kissed Milo on the top of his head and started toward the front door.

In the living room, my brother, Steven, was sleeping on the couch, sleeping under his raincoat, a pillow covering his face. So he must have had a fight with Lisha after I went to bed. When I'd left the kitchen the night before, late, after midnight, studying for a graduate entomology exam, Lisha—his girlfriend of the moment, marooned at our house for the night—was in Steven's room with him, something that wouldn't have been possible if our mother were at home. So an argument must have happened between them, not surprising with Steven.

I grabbed my raincoat from a hook by the front door, slipped a red umbrella under my free arm and turned the knob quietly so as not to wake him.

At first, when I stepped onto the front porch, shut the door behind me, adjusted the coffee and umbrella and backpack over my shoulder, I didn't see the large blue flag draped over our round wrought-iron table and stretched along the floor covering half the porch.

And then I did.

The flag was midnight blue with an eagle in profile in the center, holding sheaves of wheat in its talon. DEPARTMENT OF JUSTICE was written across the top. An oily black smudge across the fold, as if the flag had been run over by the tire of a bicycle.

My first thought was Faith.

Steven had followed me outside, sleepy-eyed, his coat wrapped around his shoulders.

"What is this is about?" I asked.

His face took on the dark, defended look he sometimes had.

"It must be a gift," he said.

A sense of dread washed over me. Steven was a lightning rod for trouble.

In those dreams you have as a child, thinking what would happen to you if your mother died or your father died—who among your family could you bear to sacrifice without dying yourself?—it was always Steven I couldn't lose if I had to choose to save one of them.

"A gift from whom?" I asked.

"I can't answer that," he said.

"Maybe it has something to do with Faith's work at the Department of Justice."

"Not likely," he said, crouching down and gathering the flag in his arms.

"What are you going to do with it?" I asked.

"Get rid of it before you come home with Julia or she'll flip out."

"Maybe it's a prank?"

"Probably guys at law school. Some of the Young Republicans who give me a hard time." He ruffled my hair.

I had started across the lawn toward the car when he called.

"I've got another op-ed piece in this morning's paper," he said.

"About what?"

"It's not very complimentary of the present administration, and

I'd be just as happy if Julia didn't know for a while. She's not going to love it."

"Julia loves *everything* you do," I said.

"She won't like this piece."

I left uneasily, Steven still standing on the porch as I pulled out of the driveway, his arms folded across his chest, his thick, black, un-tamed hair sticking out in all directions, looking frazzled as he used to look when he was a grumpy little boy.

Driving south toward Key Bridge, taking the high roads to avoid the flooded streets near the river, I couldn't get the image of the De-partment of Justice flag out of my head. Just the unlikely size of it appearing in the middle of the night, filling up our front porch.

I opened the window for air, the rain splattering across my shoul-ders. My father's old blue Toyota smelled of something rotten— probably some groceries he'd bought and forgotten about, which had slid under the seat, crowding the textbooks and papers and old newspapers and shirts that spent days on the floor of the backseat before they got to the laundry. It was difficult to put up with my par-ents' old habits.

I was an adult still living at home, and so was Steven, and to say we did it happily would not be entirely true. But I wonder now whether we weren't both grateful to have the excuse of graduate school, the expense of it, the need to conserve cash. Whether we didn't want to leave quite yet. Something about our mother's fears for the future of our family kept us close, to swell the ranks.

When I drove up to the glass factory in Alexandria, my mother was standing at the entrance smoking a cigarillo—a small, substantial woman in her late fifties, with a mass of short, wiry hair, dressed in strong colors, a mustard yellow cape, a loose-fitting purple shirt and gathered skirt and red lipstick—a Gypsy look that had its charm, suggesting a quality of character.

I stopped the car and opened the door.

"Is the parkway still underwater?" she asked, rubbing off the end of the cigarillo on the sidewalk, dropping the rest in her purse and climbing into the front seat.

"I couldn't have gotten here if the parkway were underwater, Julia." I leaned over to kiss her. "A narrow escape from near disaster."

"Don't make light of it. Floods have washed away whole towns. Read the paper."

Steven and I called our mother Julia. At a certain point, before I was out of grammar school, she decided that we were too old to call her Mama, and she'd never been maternal anyway, she said, which wasn't exactly true. She had concocted a life in which her terrors for the safety of her family were repeated over and over like prayer, as if to name the dangers might have the power to overcome them.

She was the daughter of Czech Jews who had escaped from Prague in 1941, before my mother and her sister, Faith, were born, emigrating to Chile, where their girls were raised as generic children, neither particularly Jewish nor Latin nor Czech, mainly Lustig, which was my mother's maiden name. Years later on September 11, 1973, a military coup overthrew the democratic government in Chile, General Pinochet assumed absolute power and my mother's family escaped again, emigrating to New York City, passing on to their daughters a legacy of pursuit that my mother in particular had taken to heart.

But on this morning of April 4, in the middle of a flood, her fears were not entirely unreasonable. In the long shadow of 9/11, most people in Washington, accustomed to regular warnings of possible terrorist attack, were in the grip of unspoken hostility, wary of one another, fearful of differences.

My father, a scientist with a tendency to fatalism, believed in inevitabilities.

"We're animals," he would say wearily. "And, frightened, an animal attacks."

Julia pulled down the sun visor above the passenger's seat, using the mirror to see while she brushed her hair and put on lipstick.

"Is this color too red?" she asked.

"I can't look. I'm driving."

I wasn't a good driver, too easily distracted, with no instinct for anticipation, so I had to concentrate.

Last night had been the first in years that my mother had spent the night away from home, and I could feel her assess my emotional temperature for signs of trouble.

"So everything's fine at home, yes? Just an inconvenience, this flooding."

I was wondering should I be in second gear going down the hill? Would the car skid in third, as the one in front of me had done at a stop sign?

"Everything's okay," I said.

By the time we got home, Steven would have figured out the origin of the flag, would have concluded that it was a joke from one of his friends at law school, or an angry present from the girlfriend who had preceded Lisha, or a prank played on him by some of the teenage boys in the neighborhood.

He might have told my father about the flag, and, if so, my father would have kept the news to himself, slipped it into a place beyond consciousness. Certainly he wouldn't have told my mother, who made him crazy with her imagined disasters.

"Nothing about Steven?"

"Why do you ask?" I turned up the hill toward River Road.

"I have a bad feeling," she said. "We *always* get calls about Steven."

"You *always* have a bad feeling."

I turned the radio to WTOP to check the traffic report.

"So who's at home?" Julia asked, a nervous habit, going through the list of family members, expecting—she couldn't help herself—that something might have happened to one of us in her absence.

"Everyone," I replied, driving with care across Key Bridge into Georgetown, Canal Road closed, Wisconsin Avenue, a slight rise headed north, low water rushing toward us, slippery with an oily sheen.

"At least everyone was there when I left."

"And is your father's headache better?" Julia asked, changing the subject.

"He was in the shower when I left."

"Of course he has headaches," Julia said. "Who wouldn't, using poisonous glue on his stupid airplane, keeping the doors to the hangar shut so the fumes can obliterate his brain?"

I drove slowly because of the wet streets and rush-hour traffic, which was beginning to pick up.

"Your conversation is making me nervous," I said, turning into the subdivision where our house was located, close enough to the river that streams of water rushed along the curb as we drove the winding road.

Our family lived on Newland Street in Bethesda, between Bradley Boulevard and Old Georgetown Road, a nameless subdivision of matching ranch houses on square, half-acre lots, and we'd remained here even after the family outgrew the house and my father left the National Institutes of Health, taking an appointment downtown on the faculty of the George Washington University Medical School. We couldn't find an affordable house in Washington convenient to my father's job with sufficient garden to accommodate a full-size hangar.

"I have a premonition," Julia said, rearranging herself so she could look at me.

My mother often had premonitions at night. In the morning she'd lean against the kitchen counter, warming her hands with a cup of coffee, and tell us her bad dreams while we rushed through breakfast to get to work or school on time. There was no stopping her.

"Last night I was trying to sleep in my office, which wasn't very comfortable, and I could hear the rainwater hurtling over the banks of the Potomac, taking the rocks and mud with it, and a terrible feeling came over me that the earth was sick to death of holding up all the buildings we've loaded on its surface, and I could feel what it would be like if the ground gave way and the buildings collapsed."

"That wouldn't be possible," I said.

"Consider Pompeii. A whole city buried for hundreds of years under the rubble."

"That was a volcano, Julia."

"Well?"

"We don't have volcanoes here."

Sometimes I imagined my mother lying on her back next to my father, who'd be sleeping easily, dreaming of Darwin, and she'd be going through her lists of evidence organized in the catalog of her brain. A Korean child murdered in Maine by a gang of boys mistaking her for an Arab. A Cuban mother of four killed as she entered an abortion clinic in Miami. Three unrelated people at a coffee shop in Rockville, Maryland, obliterated by a gunman because one among them wore a turban and the gunman assumed they were together.

"My duty," the gunman said when he was arrested for murder.

Then, for a few long weeks the autumn after 9/11 a Washington Beltway sniper and his brainwashed protégé traveled the inner loop from one suburb to the next in a wide circle of the city, eating in restaurants between killings, working out in gyms, using the trunk of the car as a duck blind, shooting whoever happened to come into the frame of their telescopic sight.

There must have been many nights when my mother couldn't sleep, her eyes traveling down a mental list of disasters.

I turned in to Newland Street.

"Home!" Julia said with a long sigh, as if it were a miracle we had arrived safely. And, reaching into her large bag, something between a purse and a full-size suitcase, she searched for something.

"So," she said to me, her hand deep in the bottom of the over-crowded bag, "I have a present for you, which I found during my sleepover at the factory."

My mother was always bringing presents to our family, personal gifts for no particular reason, unless it was to make up for driving us crazy.

"A treasure," she said, lifting a small black thing wrapped in a piece of toilet paper out of her bag, setting it in her lap.

I pulled in to the driveway between the hangar and the house, stopped the car and turned off the ignition, grateful that the flag was no longer on the front porch.

"Just take it," Julia said. "Don't think I enjoy sitting here in the front seat with a dead bat in my lap. It's what I do for you."

The bat, a small one, brittle, dead for some time, was perfectly intact. A pallid bat with delicate facial features and pop eyes and a fuzzy little topknot. Beautiful wings.

"I love it," I said, opening one of the wings with care. "And I don't have any bats in my room."

I had been allowed to keep everything I found—insects, living and dead, a harmless snake, some mice, a baby rat, a one-winged bird, and once a rabbit who had two litters without benefit of a mate.

My father had cut out the middle of my south-facing wall and filled it with glass, so my room became a kind of greenhouse, ripe with the thick, fetid smell of living things and dead ones.

I held my hand out in front of me to get a better look at the baby bat in his toilet-paper bed.

I had a reputation in my family as a collector, like my mother, but Julia collected stones and photographs of strangers and lists of bad news, and I collected dead things, mainly animals, although I did have plants and a few living creatures.

Our house was small and crowded. Couches covered with soft African cloth and wooden tables with books and the stones my mother had collected on a trip to Martha's Vineyard. There were primitive Andean bowls and early-twentieth-century photographs of other people's families scattered among our own family photographs on the side tables, in the bookcase, hanging on the walls.

My mother picked up photographs of people at secondhand stores and antique book- and print shops and old photography stores. Mostly posed shots, set pieces, a family group against a fixed background. But she preferred the candid photographs—an early-twenties photograph of a child in a field of high grasses, and one of two boys sitting on their haunches, straddling a railroad track, and another of a young woman, bare-breasted, her skirt lifted above her knees, standing in the river—this one had noted in Spanish on the back *"Mariana at the river. Valdivia. 1921."*

"Why do we have these pictures of strangers?" I asked her once.

"Because our family is too small," she'd replied, as if that answer should be satisfactory.

"I don't understand."

"Think, Claire," she said. "We have only seven. Too small is too small."

Later I had asked my father. "Too small for what?"

"For a baseball team," he'd replied.

I put the dead bat in the pocket of my raincoat, unlocked the front door and followed my mother to the kitchen.

Everyone was there, surprising for a Tuesday morning, and it seemed to me as if an argument had been in progress, which stopped when the front door opened.

"Why are you late for class?" my mother asked Steven, who was leaning against the sink eating cereal.

"My nine o'clock was canceled, or I'd be gone already," he said, rinsing his cereal bowl.

Julia dropped her cape over the back of a chair and pushed up the sleeves of the peasant blouse she was wearing. "What's going on here?" She stood at the sink, her arms across her chest.

"Nothing is going on," my father said.

"I feel it on my skin," she said.

I took the pallid bat out of my pocket and hung up my raincoat, saying nothing, sensing that my mother's instincts were right.

"At least you owe me some explanation about these looks passing back and forth." She turned to my father, wiping her hands on her skirt. "Say something, David."

My father was tall and slender and sometime during his growing up, he must have felt too tall, because he walked at a slight angle to the ground, as if he were always headed into the wind. He had wispy gray hair and deep, dark, heavy-lidded eyes and a smile that filled his face. His students, watching him write formulas on the black-board, remarked on the size of his hands, especially, his long fingers, with a wingspread the width of a small baby.

He was amused by my mother, grateful that she lived a life of high relief. It colored his world, and though he was inclined to a contemplative life, she filled the house with the illusion of a large family, better than the drunken, gossipy community he left in Wales, but similar.

He and Uncle Milo grew up on a failing sheep farm near Llangollen in north Wales, and when he was twenty, he came to the United States to study medicine. There was nothing for him in Wales except the sustaining chatter of the town where he was born. He met my mother on the subway in New York City, where he was studying medicine and she was a junior seamstress making costumes for the New York City Opera. When they met, she had been in the United States for ten months, and in that time both of her parents had died, one of cancer and the other of a failing heart. My father, who had grown up with a mental landscape of gray skies, weeks without the sun, noticed my mother for the wild colors she wore and her bright cheeks and funny way of speaking with her hands. They got together between Twenty-eighth Street and Lincoln Center on the uptown Seventh Avenue train, and within weeks they'd married, knowing little of each other beyond the intensity of attraction and driven by a desire for home.

In their uneasy construction of a new family, there were deep pockets, secrets guarded even from one another—especially from one another—for fear that too much knowing might unsettle the status quo.

I sat down at the end of the table, far enough away from Bernard that I didn't have to listen to him slurp his coffee.

Milo had the front page of the newspaper opened on the table and was arguing with Bernard about light—whether to keep the blinds in the room they shared up or down during the rainy month of April.

"You could go back to your *own* apartment," Milo was saying.

"That's what you tell me every day," Bernard replied.

"So pay attention," Milo said. "I must believe it."

"What's the news?" Julia asked Milo. "More floods?"

"Arson in a nightclub on H Street," Milo said, pouring himself coffee. "No deaths reported. That's the major news for the city."

Faith stood next to the wall phone, reading the food section of the paper. A slight woman, more like me than my mother in bone structure, with a kind of whimsy and abandon, a tendency to optimism.

"I'm reading about food," Faith said. "Here's a recipe for a French fish soup that you should make, Julia."

"When there's a celebration," Julia said.

"My birthday is on Saturday," Milo said.

"But you don't like fish, Milo."

"Quite correct. I hate fish. I'd like you to make beef the way you do, spicy on the outside and red in the middle. Very nice."

"Coffee, anyone?" Faith asked me, putting down the paper.

"In just a minute." I held up the bat for Faith. "First I have to put Mr. Adorable in my room."

"With dispatch, I hope," Milo said, leaning over to peer between the toilet-paper blankets.

"It's a baby pallid bat, a rarity," I said, heading toward my room to escape the tension just beneath the surface of conversation.

Milo called me back.

"Just a minute, everyone," he said, always pleased to take center stage. "Listen here. Steven has a new op-ed piece on the editorial page this morning."

I looked over at my brother, but his face told me nothing. His arms were folded across his chest, an almost smile turning his lips, an expression of mild interest in his eyes. Lisha, standing beside him, leaning against the sink, looked homicidal.

"You didn't tell me, Steven, " Julia said. "You always tell me about your op-ed pieces."

"He didn't tell anyone," Lisha said.

"I only found out last night that the *Post* was printing it today," Steven said. "And, Julia, you've been away."

"Overnight. Less than twenty-four hours. You had plenty of time to tell me."

"A full column," Milo was saying. "Very impressive. So listen up, everyone."

I took note of the room—Steven and Lisha standing behind Milo so he couldn't see them. My father had taken a chair, pulling it away from the table into a corner, isolating himself as he was inclined to do. Julia stood at attention right in Steven's line of sight, and Faith, the food page folded under her arm, leaned against the wall next to the telephone.

Only Bernard wasn't paying attention, concentrating on adding more brown sugar to his oatmeal.

Civil Rights?

The Freedom for Democracy Act (FDA2) states as its purpose the uniting and strengthening of America by providing appropriate tools to intercept and obstruct terrorism. In the name of protecting American freedom, the FDA2, enforced under the Civil Rights Division of the Department of Justice, has had, among its many successes, the following:

An Arab father living in low-rent housing with his wife and baby, is searched, beaten and robbed of personal treasures—photographs, a prayer rug, some jewelry—when he protests law-enforcement officers searching his bedroom for possible terrorists.

A young black woman with a Muslim name is detained without cause at the airport in Indianapolis, denied food and drink and an opportunity to make a telephone call.

An Israeli mother of five young children is stopped and questioned leaving a grocery store outside of Denver, Colorado, pushed into a police van and handcuffed because she meets a description of "terrorist suspect—woman, short, dark-skinned, black hair."

A Korean courier is arrested in a botched store-robbery attempt in which he is not involved but runs from the police. The arresting officer ignores the Miranda warnings and fails to inform the suspect of his rights.

"He didn't speak English, so how could I tell him his rights?" the policeman asked after the terrified courier died of an asthma attack brought on by fear.

I tried to catch Steven's attention, but he was focused beyond, looking out the window next to the driveway, no clue in his face to what he might be thinking.

"Stop reading, Milo," Faith said quietly, putting the food section of the paper on the table.

"I want to know what happens," Bernard said, suddenly attentive.

"Why did you write that piece, Steven?" Faith asked, the color gone from her face. "You've attacked my job."

"It's where you work, Aunt Faith, not what you do," Steven said.

"I work for the Civil Rights Division of the Justice Department," she said. "It's what I do."

And before anything more got said, I left the kitchen, taking my rare pallid bat in his toilet-paper bed to my room.

2

My bedroom was set up as a place of worship. Dried flowers and living plants and animal skeletons and perfectly intact insects were arranged on the tops of tables and bookcases and my bureau. I slipped the baby bat next to the skeleton of the spider monkey missing one back leg and lying on a pillow of Queen Anne's lace.

When we were small, tiny, doll-like Eva with her pale red hair had an altar to Our Mother of Somebody, maybe the Virgin—I can't remember—but the altar was on a table in a corner of her room, with a white cloth and candles and a tiny white prayer book. The object of adoration was a small, round-faced woman with wide-set eyes, in love with Jesus, Eva had said. She was painted wood, her folded shawl bloodred, her dress sapphire blue. Beside her on the dusty shrine was a stack of dried white flowers tied with purple ribbon and a faded red plastic hibiscus.

When Eva was in her bedroom, she kept the lights dim, the candles lit, incense burning—its sweet, erotic smell filling the sanctuary.

On the floor beside the altar was a bench where she knelt to pray to Our Mother and to make her offerings, usually of money, which she'd take back when she needed it—sometimes a strand of her own hair or a single jewel she'd wrenched from a glittery, inexpensive bracelet.

I was fascinated by the soft, holy quiet of Eva's room, so I copied it, making a sanctuary for my dried insects and animal skeletons and bird feathers and snakeskins with a south window full of lush flora and fauna, a Garden of Eden.

Long after Eva had given up on God, I kept my altar to the dead.

When Lisha stormed into my bedroom in her tiny short skirt and skinny red top, I was examining the fanciful green legs of my praying mantis against the white sheets of my bed.

"What happened after I left?" I asked.

"Faith went to her room, and your parents argued, and Steven defended the piece, and your father said in his deepest Welsh accent, 'Not to worry, my treasures, everything will be fine.' " She kicked off her shoes. "Exactly what you'd expect."

"Did Milo read the rest of the op-ed aloud?"

"What he read while you were in the room was enough." Lisha collapsed on the bed, her arms flung across her eyes. "I don't know *why* Steven did that."

"You hadn't read it before?"

"He doesn't show me anything he writes," she said, pulling her knees up to her chest, her eyes closed. "He must have known Faith would be furious. He's not stupid."

"It wasn't a personal attack on Faith," I said, protective of Steven by instinct.

"Don't be naïve." Lisha had a small, girlish voice, and when she was angry—and that year she was often angry with Steven—her voice trembled. "What Steven wrote is an attack on the Justice Department and Charles Whatever-His-Name-Is, the guy Faith works for. Face it, Claire. What he wrote was an attack."

"Faith and Charles Reed are friends," I said, having no sense whatever of Faith's relationship with Charles Reed, but a strong familial tendency to "sweep our troubles under the rug," as my father liked to say. "Nothing's going to happen because of an op-ed piece in the *Washington Post.*"

"To Steven or to Faith?

I didn't reply. Perhaps I didn't even believe my own convictions, but I knew that Lisha, a linear thinker with a suspicious nature, thought I was a foolish optimist and eventually would pay a price for it.

"Be serious, Claire. Something will happen to Faith's job."

"I think you're wrong. Maybe you don't realize how warm and easygoing Faith is. Everybody loves her."

Faith had come to Washington with Daniel Wendt, who was a sculptor. We had one of his pieces on the mantel in our living room—a slick, black abstraction that looked like a replica of the kidneys, titled *Young Bird in First Flight #3.*

She was pregnant with Bernard, and Daniel Wendt was already ill when they arrived, so they married just months before he died. Afterward she went to work as an assistant to a young man clerking for a justice of the Supreme Court.

The clerk was Charles Reed.

I don't know when Faith started to work in civil rights, but I do know she went to the Justice Department when I was in the sixth grade and had worked there through two administrations. When Charles Reed was appointed assistant attorney general for civil rights, he gave Faith a "plum job"—my mother's description—with a large office and her own secretary.

What I knew of Charles Reed came from Julia, whose judgments about people—and she always came to absolute, immutable judgments—were emotional. I had never met him. But Julia liked him because he'd had the romance to marry a concert pianist from Buenos Aires, who was killed in an automobile accident in Rock Creek Park when their only child, a son, was six. It was the kind of tragedy that won my mother's heart.

As far as I knew, Faith had an old-fashioned girl's relationship with Charles Reed, loyal to her employer with no particular interest in politics. I assumed the extent of her involvement with the Justice Department was a paycheck. The subject of work never came up between us. Sex was my favorite conversation with Aunt Faith, and I think it was hers with me.

But I could imagine that her soft presence in the cold, marble halls of the Justice Department must have been like spring. She was lovely in a warm, fleshy way, with a Latin's capacity for intimacy, so it was no surprise to us that Charles Reed offered her a job in the administration and an office just down the hall from his own.

Lisha crossed her legs on the bed, rubbing her eyes.

"Steven's in hot water, as your father would say."

"Meaning what?"

"The dean of the law school at GW told him to keep a low profile after some article he wrote was published in the law review, so something's going on."

"He never told us that," I said.

"He wouldn't tell you." She threw up her hands. "Just in the last few months, he's been entirely different, always distracted."

"He seems like Steven as usual to me."

"At least he still talks too much." She took her hair out of a rubber band, combing it with her fingers. "Blah, blah, blah. So many opinions!"

"That's what I love about him," I said. "He's fearless."

She shrugged, got up from the bed, patting my leg in a gesture maybe even of generosity.

"Fearless is just another definition for foolish."

"Learn to shut up," my mother would tell Steven. "Keep yourself a secret."

"You *never* shut up," Steven argued.

"At home I talk, but outside of this house I'm a closed drawer," she replied.

Our family drew strict boundaries around our lives. Except for the accident of fate that cost Bernard Wendt his left leg below the knee, we maintained the illusion of order, with rules of behavior, an accommodating point of view. "Live and let live," my father would say. This was perhaps the way of a family like ours. We wanted to fit in, to seep like water into whatever group we happened to be with, defining ourselves as particular only at home.

I could speak with any accent I heard, Spanish or French or Japanese. According to my mother, it was a matter of kindness to other people to adapt. A matter of assimilation, according to Steven.

"I suppose you're the one who saw the flag first this morning," Lisha said, shaking out her ash blond hair. "Hard to miss."

"It was stretched across the porch when I left to pick up Julia."

"Well?" When Lisha was nervous, and she was often nervous, she attacked. "Didn't you think there was something weird about the Justice Department's flag lying on your front porch?" she snapped.

"I thought it was probably a prank," I said, folding my legs under me, leaning against the headboard.

"And now what do you think, since Steven's op-ed piece attacked the Civil Rights Division of the Justice Department? And your poor aunt."

"But whoever put the flag on the porch last night wouldn't have had a chance to read the op-ed piece until this morning," I said. "People are just picking up their papers now."

"Whatever you think, that stupid flag was a warning," she said.

She raised her arms above her head, catching her reflection in the mirror.

"But nevermind," she said wearily. "I don't know a thing about Steven's private life."

"I thought that *you* were his private life?"

A dark smile flitted across her face. "No, Claire. Steven has a *real* private life."

Steven had always had girlfriends, ever since I could remember, in seventh grade and eighth grade and ninth grade and on and on, and Lisha was like all of them, pretty, slight, fair, with a kind of weariness and patience and sorrow as if, either before Steven or as a result of knowing him, her capacity to imagine her life had collapsed. Most of the girlfriends lasted a year or so, but Lisha had been with Steven since his first year of law school, so I assumed they would inevitably marry, because that was what couples did in their twenties. Not that I didn't like Lisha—she was "fine"—that's what I told Bernard, who liked to hear about romance—and she wasn't in my way with Steven.

I leaned against a chair, my stomach sinking.

"When you're with someone, you know. Lately Steven's absent even when we're together. A lot of times, I haven't a clue where he is, only that he's not at home and he's not at school." She paced the room, her hands deep in the pockets of her short skirt. "He's unpredictable. My father says he's a loose canon who's going to break my heart."

She picked up a tube of my lipstick from the dresser. Ruby Red and brand-new, a present from Julia, who was in the habit of supplying me with makeup, which I seldom used. "Yours?"

I nodded.

"Okay if I try it?"

"You may be too blond for that color."

"Better on dark skin," she agreed, checking the color in the mirror, wiping off her lips.

I was dark, with olive skin and long hair, curly when the weather was damp, and eyes too black to see the pupils. Bone thin and very tall, with my father's smile.

My mother often told me I was beautiful, but I was not. My features were too irregular—a strong nose, full lips, bottom teeth a little crooked in the front. My hair would go gray before I was thirty, as my father's had.

Lisha stood at the door, leaning against it, her small lips drawn tight as if she'd suddenly remembered something unpleasant she had to do. "I want to ask you something."

In the shadows of my room, she looked exhausted, and I felt a rush of sympathy or generosity, even of affection, toward her.

"Steven loves you. He's told me," I blurted, the words out of my mouth before I had a chance to retrieve them.

"That's not true, Claire," Lisha said. "And it's not the question I wanted to ask you."

Outside, the sky was beginning to clear, although it was still raining. Water spilled down the window in long strings, a faint rainbow visible above the trees. I sat very still on the end of my bed, weary, with a strange misgiving, watching the weather obscure the landscape beyond the glass.

For a long time, I had lived on the surface. No intimation, no sense at all of what I could become, what life would require from a woman of my disposition when the skin was cut away. A vague anticipation was the sense I had, as if I were expecting a visitor.

3

When I came back into the kitchen, Steven was gone. Probably somewhere behind the hangar, fighting with Lisha.

"Where did you hide the flag?" my mother asked, looking up from the dishes as I crossed the room.

"I didn't hide it," I said.

"Then Steven did."

My father was resting against the wall, reading the editorial page of the *Washington Post*, a habit he had, to read the paper in the kitchen but standing up, removing himself from the conversation at the breakfast table.

"What flag?" Milo asked.

Julia wiped her hands, wet from the dishes, on her skirt.

"The Justice Department flag that was delivered to our front porch this morning as a gift to Steven."

"Could we *not* have this discussion now, Julia?" My father folded the newspaper and put it on the counter.

"What discussion?" Milo asked, his long fingers fluttering in the air like birds. He had an affection for controversy, particularly familial. "And what do you mean that the Justice Department flag was delivered to our house. Who are *we*?"

"Nobody, Milo," my father said. "We are nobody."

"Well"—Milo raised his hand in a gesture of *So?*—"we must be *somebody* today."

Things happened quickly then. My father motioned to my mother, cast a look over Milo's head and the two of them headed toward their bedroom. Faith must already have left for work, and Bernard, anxious about relationships with their inevitable possibility for conflict, picked up a blueberry muffin and limped toward the room he shared with Milo, leaving Milo and me at the kitchen table.

"This family is crazy," Milo said. "Something psychotic in the genes, not from the Welsh blood. So tell me about the flag."

I hoisted my book bag over my shoulder, glanced out the window that overlooks the garden and could see, even with the foggy weather, the outlines of Steven and Lisha leaning against his car. They seemed to be having an argument.

"I don't know about the flag," I said.

My parents were fighting when I knocked on their bedroom door, but Julia's was the only voice I heard.

When I put my ear against the door, my mother was speaking in her attenuated voice, punctuating each word to make a point.

"The piece in this morning's paper is going to be the end of our family as we know it."

My father was a genius at silence.

"You *know* that, David, and I can't for the life of me understand how you *missed* a flag the size of our front yard on the porch this morning."

She went on without a beat. "You must have been working in the hangar or been in the shower or in bed with a headache and didn't know that Steven hid the flag and I had to find out about it from my sister."

She made a funny bass sound in her throat. "My poor sister!"

The door flew open just as I was about to knock again, and my mother was standing in a maroon half-slip, no bra, her wet hair in a towel, holding the oversize flag, which had been folded.

"You knew it was in your closet and didn't mention it to me in the car," she said.

"I didn't know it was it was in my closet," I replied.

"Well, Faith found it in your closet when she was borrowing your gray sweater so you must have seen the flag when you left this morning to pick me up at the factory."

"I was the one who found it." I sank down on the bed.

Beyond us my father was creating a storm, gathering papers from his desk, putting them in his briefcase.

"It's a bad omen, that flag, announcing trouble for my son."

"The bad omen is the op-ed piece, Julia," my father said. "Steven thinks it's safe in this climate to say whatever comes across his mind, and so he does."

My father put on a sweater, then another, tossing the first one on the floor of his closet.

"I suppose you're saying I encourage him."

"Not necessarily you," my father said carefully, never willing to tip the balance between them. "Both of us."

"So it's my fault Steve wrote that op-ed for which my sister will never forgive me," she said.

"I said it's *our* fault that he feels free to attack anyone he doesn't agree with, including his aunt's employer. Our fault, Julia. I'm not blaming you."

But my mother had been the one responsible.

She and Steven used to sit at the kitchen table eating chocolate chip cookies and scones—this was years ago when he was in junior high—and I'd be at the table, too, listening and listening, a ghost of a child, never involved, never invited.

"Fight," was Julia's motto for my brother. "Stand up to this teacher or that principal or the fifth-grade bully," she'd say, always pushing Steven to an outrage already deep in his nature.

He had grown up quarreling with anyone in authority, willing to say what other students didn't dare, preparing for revolution.

My mother loved that spirit in Steven, loved what was absent in my father's otherworldly, abstract, gentle way. Steven had qualities she must have felt sleeping in her own character, taking risks that she might have taken if she'd been in such a position, if she'd been younger or American born or a man.

"There's nothing worth worrying about." My father brushed away the rising conversation. "What's done is done."

Julia slipped one of her bright Mexican blouses over her head. "That's not what you said to me the other night in bed, David." She took a yellow cotton skirt out of the closet, pulling the waistband tight, struggling to button it. "What you said then was that you wished Steven would be more circumspect and compromising." She tossed a towel in the clothes hamper. "Your words, not mine."

"Whatever I said in our bedroom was private."

"Private!" my mother said. "I don't know the meaning of that word."

My father's temper seldom flared, but it did now, and he gathered up his papers, buckled his briefcase and headed out of the bedroom. "If you want to come with me, Claire, I'm leaving now."

"I'll wait for Steven," I said.

Julia was sitting at her dressing table, putting on mascara, looking back from the mirror at me sitting on her bed.

"So it'll just be you and Steven going to school together today, right?"

"And Lisha."

"But you'll drop her off at work?"

"Yes."

"When you're alone with Steven, just the two of you in the car, ask him what he's up to outside of school."

"What do you mean by that?"

"I've been wondering whether he's involved with something we don't know about."

"Like what?"

"Some political group. I know he's involved with the democrats at school, and I know he takes a left-wing position on issues, but I have this feeling there's something else going on."

"He doesn't have time for a political group as long as he's in law school," I said.

I used to be quick to deny any possibility of trouble, "a cockeyed optimist" my father said of me. But he knew better, certainly than I did, that the defenses of our particular mix of genes were fragile and that my kind of optimism was a thin shield and not to be counted on.

Julia shrugged. "Steven has time for what he has time for, Claire," she said. "I know him very well."

I didn't argue. I seldom did.

4

I sat in the backseat of the old green Ford, watching Steven's hands on the steering wheel. An urgency to everything he did, even his grip on the top of the wheel, his knuckles protruding bone white, like the knuckles of an old man, his jaw set, his foot tapping nervously on the floorboards. In the rearview mirror, I could see his black eyes and narrowed my own so he couldn't tell I was watching him.

He was talking to Lisha about this and that, whether she'd be finished work in time for a drink at Demi's Bar, whether they'd go to the Blue Ridge Mountains for the weekend, how much work he had to do, especially in criminal law. He was catching a cold.

Lisha stared out the window at the line of tract houses, their colors articulated in the gray day.

Viewed from my window in the backseat, our neighborhood had

an eerie, soundless menace—the string of rectangular houses so low to the ground they seemed in the threatening weather to sink beneath its surface, the lamps lit in the matching living rooms casting a garish yellow circle on the tiny lawns, the upstairs shades drawn as if there'd been a death. No one was on the street.

We had moved to this suburban outpost when I was eight, no longer an outpost since I left elementary school, new neighborhoods surfacing like weeds along the strip north of the city. When we were young, Julia tried to make a family of the neighbors, who were mostly visiting foreign doctors at NIH whose tenure at the government medical-research laboratories was temporary. But on Sunday nights Julia would give big suppers and push back the furniture in the living room for dancing, while the children of the neighborhood played in the kitchen a form of hide-and-seek we called "Scare Me to Dead."

And then the daughters of a local radio disc jockey shopping with their parents at Montgomery Mall disappeared, and every day on the 8:00 A.M. show, the father of the girls was on the radio pleading with his listeners for information, any information that might lead to his girls. My mother was a listener, the radio always on at seven when we came into the kitchen for breakfast. But the girls were never found, and the dinner dances in our house ended.

"Why no more parties?" I asked my mother.

"Nobody stays in Washington for very long," she said. "No point in getting to know anyone."

The air inside the hot, sticky room of the car was thick with silent argument, and though I must have sensed, behind Steven's talk of incidentals, the conversation that wasn't taking place, I was more or less in the dark about the subtle hostilities of relationships. I needed to learn cunning, and even last year I must have known that its absence was my protection against the truth.

When I think of myself then, at twenty-two still a virgin with a sense of my own soul's purity, the picture I have is one my mother keeps beside her bed. In it I am seven, already lanky and tall, wearing a white ruffled pinafore, which is too tight and too short, above my knees. My hair is braided with ribbons, an expression on my face, with its too-large nose and full lips and coal-black eyes, that I can only describe as otherworldly.

"Claire's looking at heaven," my mother would say, not without irritation, giving weight to the word "heaven" clicking her tongue in the back of her throat. "She's too good for this world."

Steven stopped the car at St. Vincent's Day Care Center, where Lisha worked, watching while she got out, put up her umbrella against the light rain still falling and walked away without saying good-bye, down the long cement path, up the steps to the front door of the main building, a square-columned black stone building with the bleak suggestion of an asylum about it.

"Get in the front and talk to me," he said after Lisha had disappeared inside the building.

I climbed over and pushed the seat back to accommodate my long legs.

Steven had a way of clenching his fists so his nails made little slices on his palms, which bled. It was clear by the thin sweep of blood at the top of the steering wheel that he had just done that.

"Are they very angry?" he asked when I had settled beside him and fastened my seat belt.

"Dad is," I said. "He left the house in a temper."

"I didn't think about Faith when I was writing the op-ed. I know it's hard to believe, but I didn't." He was tapping the steering wheel in time to his own voice.

"I don't ever think about Faith working at the Justice Department, only sitting in the kitchen in bare feet with her hair down, drinking tea with Julia," I said. "She's not a working kind of woman. She just goes to work."

"That's probably why I didn't think about her job when I did the piece," Steven was saying. "I was doing research on the implications of the Freedom for Democracy Act and ran across these stories about what happened to people when the law enforcers found them, and the stories were so terrible that I wrote in a heat and thought about nothing but these poor people. It was stupid of me."

"Nothing's going to happen," I said, but I must have been wary that morning. Any sign of change in my small world had the effect of a stun gun. My mind went white. "Faith never stays angry," I said.

Steven shook his head. "Unlike Dad."

"He doesn't stay angry either. He just bolts when he's upset," I said. "He did this morning."

"He almost ran over Mr. Denver picking up his morning paper in his hurry to get to the office."

In trouble, my father would leave, maybe only as far as the airplane hangar, but a quick exit was his solution to every problem.

My father's research at the National Institutes of Health was in the National Institute of Neurological Diseases and Strokes, and his special interest was in ALS, called Lou Gerhig's disease. When I was about ten, before the disc jockey's daughters disappeared at Montgomery Mall, a young single woman with ALS on whom my father was trying an experimental drug died. She had been at NIH for months, and in the course of that time her only child, a boy about twelve, had become attached to my father.

It was early June, the windows open, a damp breeze blowing through the room, and we were having dinner at the kitchen table when my mother brought up the boy. He never had a name that I remember, referred to by my father as "the boy," as "the orphan boy" by my mother.

"I would like to tell the orphan boy we *will* adopt him, David. I want to say yes."

It was the first Steven and I had heard of the boy, and in retrospect Julia's choice for bringing up the conversation must have been to involve us in the private argument. We fell quiet, listening carefully, pretending to eat.

Julia was reasonable, quieter than usual in her defense. "There are only five of us with Milo, and the boy could be happy with us."

"The answer is no," my father said, already out of his chair, taking his half-finished meal to the sink.

"But think of it, David," my mother was saying as my father headed for the front door. "We have such a small family."

By the following week, my father had resigned his post at NIH to be a professor of medicine at George Washington University.

"Because of the boy?" Steven had asked our mother.

"Ask him," Julia said.

But Steven wouldn't dare.

We drove across town taking the back streets. Steven turned the radio up, and we listened to the WTOP report on the weather:

"Some reports suggest that an underwater explosion could have caused the Potomac to rise above the banks, but that's conjecture," the weatherman said. *"Nothing confirmed."*

Steven turned the dial to all-music.

"Lisha worries too much," he was saying. "And that makes her angry, and then we fight, usually about something there's no reason to worry about."

"About the flag?"

"The flag, the op-ed pieces, the professors, the arguments I write in the *Law Review*. Everything upsets her." He fiddled with the dial, looking for WPFW 89.3 FM Blues.

"Don't you love her?"

"I don't know if I love her," he said. "I have too much in my head."

I used to have a soft-petaled view of romance, as if love were inspiration, arriving in a rush and by surprise, and I believed that such a feeling would eventually come to me as a kind of visitation.

I tucked my feet under and opened the window a crack so the light rain misted my face. "I can imagine that sometime I'll fall in love and marry and probably have a baby and teach in a university biology department somewhere. Maybe New York."

Ever since we were small and first moved to Bethesda, we had talked about New York. We begged our mother to promise we'd move back after the school year, after the next school year or the next, telling our classmates that each year would be our last at Bethesda Elementary and then we'd be moving home. For Steven it was the elevators in New York—punch "1" and you're on the ground floor, out the door, on the street, the street crowded with people, the shops open, the coffeehouses with doughnuts and cookies in glass cases.

For me New York was Steven, who was allowed to take me out alone, around the block, stopping at the deli for juice, pressing our noses against the window of the toy store, passing the children in strollers with their parents, harnessed in while I walked free as summer along Columbus Avenue with my brother.

"I love New York," I said, hoping for a promise out of our childhoods, some permanent commitment from Steven.

I wiped the dampness off my face with the sleeve of my jacket and closed the window. We had talked about moving back many times, even recently, certainly in the last year. Steven would go back after law school and take the bar and become a public defender. I would follow when I got my doctorate, and our parents would retire to a small apartment on the Upper West Side. My father could find a part-time teaching job someplace or practice medicine, and Julia would be a freelance designer, and we'd all be back where we started, going to the Jersey shore for summer vacations.

"I thought we talked about New York just this year," I said. "You were going to go to finish law school and then take a job there."

"I need to be in Washington," he said. "Too much is happening."

It was the conspiratorial moment my mother had hoped I would have with Steven, just the two of us driving together, secrets pouring into the void between us. But I was consumed by my own yearning for something irretrievable—some feeling of *home* agitating like floaters in the eye or the taste of salt.

I sank back in my seat, turning my face away, suddenly weepy.

Just last summer we'd talked about New York, how he might live in the city and I'd get a job at a small college in the East, how our children would play together in the summers.

"So *here* is home?" I asked.

"Here is home."

We were stopped at a light then, and he looked over at me with a kind of sadness.

"You're too smart to want what's over, Claire," he said quietly, as if he didn't intend for me to hear him.

It made me angry. It makes me angry now, because he doesn't know that I've become a different person than I was that morning as we skirted the flooded streets of downtown Washington.

I wrapped my arms around my knees, my knees under my chin, my head resting at the bend. My body felt like the crispy cloak the seven-year locust leaves behind when he dies, as if my insides had evaporated in the air and I had disappeared.

"We're different people," he said.

He was probably wondering how he could explain to me that the world as I found it was only in my head, that I couldn't live forever in a sanctuary with animal corpses as holy objects.

"I'm a biologist," I said coolly, as if guessing at his thoughts. "I know about death, if that's what you're saying."

The windows were open just enough for moving air to blow the hair on the top of our heads, blues on the all-music station, Steven tapping his fingers in rhythm on my arm. Something casual and confident about his gesture that moved me, and I wanted this moment to last, just the two of us trapped in the cocoon of the car, an argument aborted, circling the streets for a clear path to our destination.

Steven pulled in to the parking lot, turned off the car, got out, and we slung our book bags over our shoulders, heading for the cement steps to the campus, a spread of buildings in the middle of the city.

"Coffee?" he asked.

I checked my watch. "I'll be late for class." I said. I could barely keep pace with him, although I had longer legs.

"Then we'll meet in the library at five as usual." He lit a cigarette.

We headed down Twenty-first Street toward the river, cutting across the traffic to the other side. A group of people walking in our direction knew Steven by name, and he waved, and a law professor stopped to ask him about the op-ed piece in the *Washington Post*, saying he liked the piece, thought it was smart and daring.

We were stopped at a light crossing G Street, and he leaned against me with his weight as if he'd lost his balance.

"Smart and daring! Not bad." Steven rested his head on my shoulder.

"Are you worried about trouble?" I asked, surprised at the sudden softness of his gesture.

"I'm not a fool."

The light had turned green, and we crossed the street to Lisner Hall, where my biology classes were held.

"It's not the flag, if that's what you're thinking. That was a gift, and

I'm glad to have it," he said, shrugging off the conversation, and I didn't know at the time whether he meant it or not, but I expect now that he did not.

He reached over and gave me a puff of his cigarette. I took it, although I don't smoke, something conspiratorial in the gesture and intimate.

"So I'll see you in the main library at five?"

"You know, Steven," I said with a flush of emotion, "I'm completely happy when you're around."

He gave my chin a gentle box and smiled. "If you're not in the library at five, I'll meet you in New York," he said, and I turned to hurry up the steps to biology.

5

My mailbox in the biology office was full of junk mail—announcements of lectures and picnics, special makeup sessions, a message from the registrar about freshman grades, a note from one of my students about missing class and a message from Faith saying she would meet me for lunch at one o'clock in the school cafeteria.

I wasn't surprised. We often met for lunch in the cafeteria for "sex talks," as Faith called them, and she would tell me about her affair with the married photographer, and I would listen.

Probably this afternoon she'd want to talk about Steven's op-ed piece and how angry she was at him for having written it. I knew that my parents were upset, knew it had been foolish of Steven to attack the department where Faith worked, but I was an expert at denial. This would "blow over," as my father often said.

I called Faith's office at the Justice Department, left a message on her voice mail that I'd meet her at one and told her I was full of despair and needed one of our sex talks about her love affair.

I was a teaching assistant in my first year of a Ph.D. program, and my particular interest was evolutionary biology. As a child I went with my family to Tivoli Gardens in Copenhagen during the summer months when the dusk turns silver and lasts all night, and the glittering lights of Tivoli are painted across my memory like a Chagall, where the ordinary life of the village is happening in the sky. That was the kind of magic I had discovered in biology, as if the study of life was a kind of Tivlovian circus and I'd been invited to live inside the gates.

For a beginning student in evolutionary biology, the *purpose* of life is simple. The simplicity of it pleased me, although it reveals perhaps a childish intelligence to confess that I was comforted by a system in which the purpose includes only the objectives of *survival* and *reproduction.*

But I liked the implicit clarity, the ongoing narrative of natural selection, which like a soap opera resurfaces season after season, the end of each segment a hook for a new beginning.

To say it plainly, as I then believed it was and told my students: If we assume in the complexity of human life the simplicity of biology, each one of us has a particular set of genes. If we fail to survive or fail to reproduce, that original set of genes is kaput.

I had a casual way of speaking to my freshman class while I was teaching.

"Suppose DDT comes to Toledo," I'd begin, "and in the process of zapping the mosquitoes, which is its job, it zaps as well a particular gene, and people with that gene wither on the spot or get cancer of the this or that, one kind of death or another. But the people lucky enough to survive have a gene that resists the DDT, a CIA secret-intelligence kind of gene that changes the genetic information to a different recipe. And those survivors *reproduce.* Ergo, over a long period of time, the population of Toledo shifts to one in which every citizen is resistant to DDT."

No genetic variation, *no* evolution, I'd say to my students. And for genetic variation we need *mutation* and *sex*. Mutation comes from mistakes in the cell's copy machine, creating an altogether new gene. Sex, just as important and much more entertaining, creates a new combination of old genes.

Get busy, I'd say to them. No evolution and we're history.

Last year when all of this was happening, I used to sit in my room, cross-legged on my bed so I could see through the plants in the south-facing window across to the hangar, and imagine my life as a woman.

The hangar was where Steven went with Lisha when no one was at home, although Steven and I never spoke about it. We never spoke of sex at all, except once he did ask me had I ever been with a man, and I didn't reply, wishing to say yes although the answer would have been no.

I was anxious about myself. I couldn't understand why I was afraid of *being* with men. I was always thinking about them— someone from biochemistry, a man with curly hair and a cleft chin who I'd seen at the market, a boy in Steven's law-school class, exactly my height with pale, pale blue eyes. Crushes I'd take into bed, sometimes waking in the middle of the night with a sense of presence beside me, surprised to find that the bed was empty, as if I believed my imagination of sufficient power to create a lover out of daydreams.

Eva had been with men since we were sophomores in high school—"indiscriminately," she'd tell me. "A product of my Catholic girlhood," she'd say.

And when we were in high school, I'd pretend to more adventure than I'd had.

By the time I went to college, there had been only deep kisses, a boy's grip on my tailbone pressing me against his groin, his hands sliding along the sides of my breasts. And I'd pull away, breathless with a bewildering mix of terror and desire, half sick, as if, like the poor male praying mantis, I could die of sex.

After class I checked my messages in the office I shared with other teaching assistants. *"Four unheard messages"* were recorded, but it was almost one o'clock, so I replaced the receiver and didn't listen to them.

I got to the cafeteria just before one and waited.

I was Faith's confidante, I suppose. She had no daughter of her own, and my mother showed little interest in and occasional criticism of her affair with the married photographer, and, living a secret life as she was, Faith must have had a need for a sympathetic friend. Something I now understand. I was a likely friend. An excellent listener, too inexperienced to have an opinion and pleased to be let into the intimate life of so seductive a woman as I thought my aunt to be, although I had no way to measure seductiveness.

By one-thirty Faith still had not arrived. I made another call to her office, and no one answered except voice mail. I got a salad and a Diet Coke and sat at a table in the window directly across from the entrance to the cafeteria so she couldn't miss me if she came.

At two I left for biology lab.

I've a capacity to put out of mind anything I don't wish to think about, but I was alarmed that Faith had not come to lunch.

I had time before lab to check the messages in my office again, but I walked past the door without opening it, picked up some printouts in the biology office, and went to lab.

When I was young, I had a habit of hiding. Something would upset me, something minor. Sometimes I couldn't even remember what it was. But when it happened, I'd disappear under the skirted table where the photographs of strangers were kept or into the broom closet or under a bed, usually my parents' bed, but always close at hand. And tall as I am, I was able to make myself small enough that no one could ever find me. I never ran away from home, although Eva used to run away to her Aunt Vera's and Steven ran away, taking me with him to the drugstore in his red wagon.

If trouble was brewing, I'd hide at home, and even then, as recently as last year, my instinct in conflict was short-distance flight. I wanted to be invisible but never too far from the source.

Which was how I felt that afternoon during biology lab, dissecting a fetal pig.

Three more messages had come since morning when I finally checked my office voice mail.

The first one was from Julia at 10:00 A.M. *"Where are you?"* The phone clicked off.

"Claire. I have to speak to you, pronto. Call as soon as you get this message." It was Julia again.

The third call was from my father asking me to call my mother at work. In his second call, he asked me to stop by his office before I went to the library to meet Steven at five.

When I arrived at my father's office, it was close to five and he was on rounds at the hospital across the street, and I suppose I was stopping by his office for reassurance and called my mother because he wasn't there.

Julia was in a temper.

"This is the worst day of my life," she said, not for the first time. "There was the op-ed piece, the flag, and now the computer has lost one of my designs."

I had adopted silence as a matter of course when Julia was on a tear.

"So what did Steven say about his extracurricular life when you asked him this morning?"

"I haven't mentioned it yet," I said. "I'll see him in the library."

"Fourteen people at work—fourteen of them—made a remark

about Steven's piece this morning, and these are glass workers who don't read the op-ed page. Your father and I are furious."

"No one said anything to me," I said.

"Well, plenty of people spoke to your father about it, and I've called Faith to check the temperature at her job—if she's still got one. I must have called her ten times so far, and she hasn't returned my call."

I had thought I might tell Julia that Faith had missed our lunch, but I changed my mind.

"That's why it's important for you to find out what Steven is up to besides law school. I have extrasensory perception, and I see problems."

"I'm actually calling about dinner, thinking I might go over to Eva's."

"Milo's cooking, for what that's worth," Julia said. "I've got to finish this project and won't be home until eight." She stopped for a moment, spoke to someone in her office, answered another telephone. I could hear her tell the caller that the order would be ready by Monday, and then she was back on the phone with me.

"You need to be at dinner tonight. The family needs to come together."

I hesitated. This was exactly the conversation I didn't want to have.

"Stormy weather," she said, my father's expression. He had a habit of humming the tune to "Stormy Weather" during arguments with Julia.

"Okay," I said. "I'll be there."

"Leave your father a note and ask him to call me when he gets back to his office."

I could tell she was trying to separate the sound of alarm from her voice, forcing herself to use the word "ask" instead of "tell."

I said I would, then hung up and called Milo.

The part of Milo that wasn't a crybaby and complainer was the part where he got to be a musician, the part I loved—generous and funny—and that was the Milo I got on the telephone.

This Milo was making lamb stew with garlic and rosemary and red wine, "roasted potatoes, very crisp on the outside, soft on the inside, like Welsh potatoes," he said, "and slivers of carrot. Julia will love it."

In this humor Milo was fond of my mother.

"If I die this afternoon," Milo was saying with good cheer, "I want you to remember me as a musician and a cook, drink a toast to me at family dinners. 'For Milo Frayn,' you'll say, 'a musician first and then a master of lamb stew from his native Wales.'"

"Are you expecting to die this afternoon?" I asked, amused.

"I'm not expecting to die ever. But 'the readiness is all,' I think."

I giggled and made a kissing sound in the receiver, since Milo's life was short on kisses, and hung up.

It was almost five o'clock, the time when I planned to meet Steven in the library, so I wrote a note to my father, and just as I was about to head down the steps and down the street to the library, the telephone rang.

It was Faith.

"I thought David would be back from class by now," she said.

"He's on rounds with the interns," I said. "I thought we were supposed to have lunch."

There was a long silence, time for me to look outside my father's window, where a little girl, not more than seven, with her umbrella up, her backpack on her shoulders, was tripping over a curb, and as she fell, the force of the wind picked up her umbrella, turned it inside out and blew it across the courtyard.

"Faith?"

"I'm still here."

And very slowly, as if she had to imagine the words one by one before she could speak them, she said, "I was calling your father to tell him I've been terminated."

"Terminated?"

"Fired."

Although I remember many of the details of what happened in April of last year, I cannot imagine myself in the scenes.

When we were young, Julia used to repeat, like a mantra of lost causes, "If only I'd known then what I know now," as if knowing were sequential and fixed in time. I'd like to think that we're born with the capacity to *know* as part of our genetic road map, but the willingness to see clearly is something else, a matter of character anticipating the future.

I believed intellectually in change and my ability to adapt to it, but emotionally I didn't trust that I had the capacity.

6

When I arrived in the reading room at the table where Steven and I always sat, he wasn't there. He'd left his books on the table but not his backpack, and there was a note on top of his constitutional-law text.

"Be back soon. A couple of things I need to do before we go home today. S"

I took off my jacket, unpacked my books, headed to the ladies' room, and by the time I got back, a couple of people—but not Steven—had sat down at the table we usually had to ourselves. One of them had moved Steven's stack of books closer to mine, and they'd fallen over, spilling his note cards, which he kept for exams, so I stacked them and put them back. I glanced at his calendar, which had been under the constitutional-law book, something I wouldn't ordinarily do, but in the back of my mind, where I shoved everything I didn't want to remember under a little fold of white matter, hoping it would get lost, I remembered Julia's request.

April 4:

11 am   See Professor Raab.
11:30   Take *Low Profile* piece and leave with the dean's sec'y.
12   Meet D—take *Law Review.*
1   Constitutional-law seminar.
4   Finish article for *Law Review* on justice vs. the law.
     Check mailbox for bad news.
5   Meet C in library. Lisha for drinks? Call early.
7   Home with C unless . . .

I made a mental note to ask him about D and what he meant by the "bad news" in his mailbox and why the word "unless"? Was he coming home for dinner or not?

I didn't plan to tell him that Faith had been fired from her job. It was very bad news for our family, and I had no idea how Steven would react. I used to think I knew him perfectly, my brother, my beloved brother and dearest friend, but I was no longer sure of him or of myself.

When Steven came up behind me, I was imagining what would happen when we arrived at home for dinner, and Faith was there and poor bewildered Bernard and my parents, still angry. Would Faith tell Steven, and what would he say to her?

"Where were you?" I asked.

"Errands," he said. "I needed a book at the bookstore and stopped by a bar to talk to a friend. And I called Faith to apologize for any trouble I might have caused her with the op-ed."

"What did she say?"

"She was out," he said.

Surely there'd be a fight in the kitchen tonight when we got home, and tears and recriminations. My father would go to the hangar to work, and I'd go to my room, and so would Faith, and Julia would stand by the sink, a dish towel over her shoulder, announcing the future to the remaining family as if it were in her absolute control.

Steven was restless, moving his books around, stacking and restacking them, fumbling with his papers, checking his watch.

"What time is it?" I asked, responding to his nerves.

"Six o'clock, later than I thought," he said. "And my concentration's shot, so I'm thinking of getting a beer."

"I'll get a beer with you if you want."

I started to close my books, aware that he was scrutinizing me, his mouth tight, so the dimple at one corner of his lips deepened in a small depression.

"What's the deal?" he asked. "You're so jumpy."

"You're the one who's jumpy."

He had opened his calendar, crossing off the list.

"What did you mean by 'home unless'?" I asked. "Unless Lisha?"

"Checking out my calendar, were you?" he asked.

"It fell open. I didn't open it."

"I always write 'unless' after 'home for dinner.' "

We usually ate dinner together by candlelight at the long wooden table in the kitchen with music playing on the radio. It was a condition of living in the house, Julia had said, when Milo and Faith and Bernard moved in. She made a ceremony of it.

"So be here for dinner," she'd say to Steven and me when we left in the morning for the university. "Who knows how many dinners are in our future?"

Steven was picking up one law book and then another, unable to settle, chewing on the eraser at the end of his pencil, cracking his knuckles. And I wonder now if he had a sixth sense of how the rest of the day would go, a feeling of cold air across his back, a coming darkness.

"*Unless* something better comes up, is what I meant," he said, opening a notebook, his chin in his fist, and finally we both settled into our work. Or he did.

I must have dozed off, my face against the plastic surface of the entomology text, when Steven woke me up.

"I lost track, and it's nearly seven," he said, slinging his backpack over his shoulder.

I stood and stretched, gathering my books and papers, stuffing them into the backpack, following him out of the reading room.

"You're always in such a hurry," I said, my hand on his arm as he rushed down the stairs.

We stopped to check our books with security at the main entrance.

"Don't I know you?" the guard asked, looking at Steven.

"I study here every night," Steven said.

The guard was checking through his law books, looking in the bottom of his bag.

"Are you a soccer player?"

"A law student. You must have me mixed up with someone else."

"You look like that guy Luis Lucero. You know him?"

"The goalie. I know who you mean."

The guard handed him back his books, and Steven knelt down,

stuffing them in the backpack, zipping the bag. I remember that particularly, because I noticed for the first time that he was getting a nest of gray hair around the crown of his head.

"So that's who you look like, Luis Lucero," the guard said. "If you get tired of law, maybe you should try soccer. You've got the right build for a goalie."

This amused the guard, and he laughed hard.

The entrance to Gelman Library was located on H Street, just below ground level, approached several steps down from the sidewalk.

"So I was thinking of us at the Jersey shore," I went on as we left the guard's desk and headed to the exit. "We weren't digging on the beach as I usually think of us doing, but we were headed into the ocean."

I put the hood of my raincoat up.

"Did we ever swim in the Atlantic Ocean?" I asked.

"I swam with Dad." Steven pushed open the heavy front door, and I followed him outside into the gathering weather. "I don't think you *ever* went swimming." He held the door for a group of students. "You hated the water."

The sky had darkened overhead, a light rain falling, and in the distance a storm was moving in the direction of the campus.

"Well, in my daydream you were about to take me swimming in the ocean with you."

"Oh, Claire," Steven laughed. "I should have taken you swimming whether you liked to swim or not."

For a moment we stood at the bottom of the steps, looking up at the campus—rush-hour traffic at a standstill, umbrellas weaving like the colored circles of a kaleidoscope above the streets lined with brownstone row houses and concrete buildings built in the seventies and dark brick blocks of classroom buildings—a sour smell of late afternoon in the rain, the sound of a helicopter overhead reporting on traffic.

I was scrambling around in the bottom of my book bag, searching under my books for an umbrella, Steven walking up the steps ahead of me, talking to an acquaintance about an assignment for class. The steps were full of students going to the library to study after their classes or leaving for night classes or home, racing to beat the inclement weather. A large crowd was milling on the steps and on the sidewalk above.

I finally found the folded red umbrella at the bottom of my bag, pulled it out and was starting to open it when I heard a sound somewhere close at hand—then Steven's voice—something like "Oh" or "No" was what he said.

I turned in his direction, and as I did, he seemed to fall slow-motion into open space and stunned as if to death, I watched him pitch backward—like a duffel bag the way he rolled toward me, falling and falling down the library steps, his body gathering speed, until finally, time like an accordion folded in on itself, he landed facedown next to where I was standing his arms splayed in a T on the cement at the bottom of the stairs.

THE LIFEGUARD CHAIR

My caterpillar died this morning of my ninth birthday in the grassy shoe box I had made for her. In sorrow and shame, I have put her on a piece of blue silk as an apology, because under my care she failed to become a butterfly.

I became a biologist when I was six, waiting for my father at his office across the hall from a lab where the students were dissecting cats. The cats had been cut open straight down the middle, their flat, furry skin pulled tight, secured with pins on the table so the students could examine their organs.

I crossed the hall, climbed up on a stool next to the professor to watch the cat spread out in front of me, pregnant with full-term kittens that one of the students took out of her belly and laid on the table for closer examination.

"I'd like to take one home," I said to the professor, overcome with longing for a fetus.

"What will you do with it, Claire?" the professor asked.

"I'll look at it," I said.

"But it's not going to grow any bigger, you understand that."

"It's a dead kitten," I replied matter-of-factly.

And so it happened that one of the dead kittens, gray with a splash of white on her face, was put in a clear jar filled with formaldehyde and given to me.

Much of the story of what got said in the biology lab that afternoon was my father's, who wasn't there. What I do remember was my pure desire for that perfect kitten, which sits in its jar on my bureau dresser along with the skeleton of a spider monkey I was given and the head of a cobra and now my poor caterpillar on her piece of blue silk.

C.F., age 9

Dead caterpillar with butterfly wings

III.

APRIL 5: MUTATIONS

Five o'clock in the morning, and the lamb stew still sitting on a low flame had shrunken to a black rock at the bottom of the pot. No one noticed the smell of burning.

In the kitchen Faith leaned against the wall next to the telephone, fielding the calls that had been coming in all night. Lisha Berg was sitting next to Milo, her hands folded in her lap. No tears. I wanted her to sob, to fall on the floor and scream and shout his name. Eva had called Lisha from the hospital, but by the time she arrived through the swinging doors of the emergency room, the doctors were telling us that Steven was dead.

I have no memory from the time Steven was shot until the doctors told us that he had died. And then, for hours until fear overtook me with a kind of centripetal force taking me with it body and soul, I remember everything as if it were permanently stored in my brain between the pages of a pop-up book.

I moved my chair away from the kitchen table so I wasn't sitting beside Bernard, whose high-pitched voice jarred my nerves, but I could hear his whispered conversation with Milo.

"What're we going to do, Milo?" he was asking.

"Nothing. We are going to do nothing," Milo said. "Rest and get ready."

"Get ready for what?"

"For people. They'll be arriving as soon as it gets to be morning."

"People." Bernard rested his head on his folded arms. "What kinds of people? Friends?"

"Bernard?" Milo said.

"Yes, Uncle Milo?"

"You know how you said 'I can't believe it' over and over again when you heard about Steven?"

"I meant it," Bernard said, lifting his head. "I can't believe it."

"Well, don't say it anymore."

Sometime in the middle of the night, my father went to the hangar, leaving the rest of us in the kitchen waiting for daylight, waiting for the neighbors and friends and colleagues who would begin to arrive at dawn with food.

My father left because he couldn't bear to listen to Julia's grief.

Initially her response took the form of questions about the last hour of Steven's life. How had he looked that afternoon, what had his mood been, his tone of voice. She asked me to repeat exactly what had happened, what had been said between us, as if in the retelling a language might be discovered that could bring him back to life.

"So you were sitting at one of the tables on the second-floor reading room of the library."

I nodded.

"How was it? Were you sitting side by side?"

"Steven was at the end of the long table and I was beside him," I said.

"Who else was there?" Julia asked.

"I don't remember."

"Graduate students? People you knew?"

"I didn't notice. We weren't alone. I know that. I didn't recognize any of the other students, or I would have said hello."

"And then what happened?"

"I was studying for my entomology exam and got sleepy and fell asleep on my arms and had a dream about the Jersey shore and going swimming with Steven."

"You never went into the water on the Jersey shore," Julia said.

Faith threw her head against the wall and covered her eyes. "Please, Julia."

"I won't shut up, if that's what you're suggesting," my mother said.

"Swimming was a dream," I said patiently.

Julia's eyes were wide and dark and unblinking, and I must have thought I had to do exactly what she asked of me or she could fall apart.

"So then you got your books together and went through security to have them checked, and you left the library by the main door and were standing at the bottom of the steps." She didn't take a breath.

"Yes."

It was the third time I had repeated the whole story, and it had come to seem necessary for me to hear my own voice like an incantation, repeating and repeating until the events of that night thinned to a bearable weight inside us.

"Then Steven walked to the top of the steps at the main entrance to the library, and there were many people, mostly students, no friends that I remember." I was whispering. "And the weather was getting stormy, and I stopped to find my red umbrella, which was in the bottom of my book bag under the books, and then I heard a noise, maybe a kind of pop, but not loud, and Steven said something like 'Oh' or 'No,' as if he'd had a surprise."

"And then?" she asked.

"He fell."

"Straight down the steps?"

"He rolled." I was chewing on the end of my index finger and must have bitten through the skin, a salty taste on my tongue. "I don't remember any more. Not the ambulance or the hospital or Eva telling me what had happened or Lisha coming or you and Daddy arriving in separate cars. Nothing until the doctors came in to tell us."

"Other people saw what happened, Julia," Faith said gently. "We'll find out more today."

"Someone said that Steven fell onto his stomach and the blood from his head or nose or wherever it was coming from left an imprint on the asphalt in the shape of a palm. That's what I was told in the hospital. It should still be there."

Lisha put her fingers in her ears.

From the bedroom to which he'd escaped while my mother was grilling me, Milo called out that something was burning. He could smell it, and it was making him sick.

"Burning?" Julia asked. "Why is something burning?"

Faith crossed the room, turned off the burner, lifted the top of the pot and looked in.

"Dinner," she said.

The politely insistent reporters were turned away until morning, and so were the police, with whom we had already spoken briefly at the hospital and would speak to for many more hours in the weeks ahead.

A small film crew from a local television station arrived in the dark. I didn't look out the window to see them, but Milo said they had stationed themselves on the other side of the street and were filming people as they arrived. Reporters from the *Washington Post* and the *New York Times* came at daybreak, but none of us had the heart to speak to them.

Mr. Denver stood in the garden of his blue ranch house and took on the role of informer for the neighborhood, with what my father later described as excessive enthusiasm.

My father's medical colleagues arrived at dawn. The dean of the law school came with several other professors, students from Steven's classes, some of whom I knew, friends of Steven's, friends from high school kept arriving. There were many strangers. The story of the Department of Justice flag spilled through the room with gathering momentum. There was muffled conversation about the op-ed piece in the morning paper. A reporter asked my father if he could see the flag, but by morning the FBI, called in because of the possibility that Steven had been assassinated, had taken the flag away as evidence.

Julia stood at the kitchen sink—a dish towel hanging off her shoulder—retelling the story of the last hour of Steven's life for her friends or friends of Steven's or his professors, anyone else willing to listen.

By six in the morning, the house was full of people—food piling up on the kitchen table, the smell of coffee and honey cakes. The house trembled with soft conversation floating through the rooms.

At some point Lisha got up from the table and went down the hall to Steven's bedroom, and I followed her, slipping across the kitchen and into my own room.

The room was hot. It had been closed all day and was heavy with the smell of animals, the musty odor of fowl, the putrid stench of mice. I had never noticed the smell before—nor the squeaking and chirping and scratching of their hunger. Now the familiar room that I had created out of the longings of my childhood was unbearable.

I lay down on my back, crossed my ankles, folded my hands across my stomach and closed my eyes against the complaints of the pushy white rat, the bird cries, the squeaking of the hungry mice, my mother's unstoppable talking rising over the sounds of sympathetic voices. And from the kitchen, even with coffee brewing, the burned smell of last night's dinner.

When my father came in and sat down on my bed, lunch was being served by the neighbors.

"What time is it?" I asked.

"Noon," he said.

Hours and hours had passed. It ought to be tomorrow, I thought. Years from now. Time had a laborious way of moving and stopping like an old bus stuck in traffic. I wished I could suddenly age.

My father put his hand against my cheek. "Claire?"

"I'm not talking," I said.

In the lamp glare, he looked terrible. His face, ashen and soft with folded flesh, had fallen in on itself. In only a matter of time, he, too, would be dead. And my mother. This flimsy house demolished by new owners wanting a more elaborate place, building one from scratch.

In a short time, only a bus stop away, it would be as if our family had never occupied this space or any place on earth. A vanished tribe. Not even our bones would remain.

"I won't be coming out of my bedroom." I pulled my covers up under my chin. "And don't send Julia in to talk to me."

Eva came instead. Eva had learned something about death, being a Catholic. She lay down on the bed beside me, her head on the same pillow, lining her tiny body up next to mine so we were touching shoulder to shoulder, wrist to wrist.

"Do you want to know what I know?" she asked. "It's factual, about how Steven died and when and what he knew about the shooting."

"I only want to know the facts." I was carelessly assembled, as if the slightest movement of my body would destroy me.

"Just tell me to stop if it's not what you want to hear." She turned on her side, balancing on her elbow, facing me. "At about seven-fifteen last night, Steven was standing on the top step of the main entrance to the Gelman Library and someone—maybe in an academic building across the street from the library or just behind the construction of a new addition—someone at close range, with what the police believe might have been a Beretta nine-millimeter with a silencer, shot him in the head."

Eva took a breath, checking my response.

"And then what?"

"He felt something for a millisecond, as if a pebble had hit him in the temple, but by the time he reacted—sort of an 'ouch' is probably how it felt—he was gone."

"Dead?"

"No. Gone to the world. Unconscious. He died at eight-fifteen on the operating table, almost as soon as the doctors had scrubbed and were about to start surgery to alleviate the swelling on his brain."

The ambulance had come quickly, Eva told me. The medics were excellent. Steven was on the operating table in less than thirty minutes.

"No chance, Claire," Eva said, her voice solid and without softness, for which I was grateful.

"So it was bad luck."

Eva hesitated. "Yes, bad luck," she said.

Eventually, after Eva went home, I left the bedroom, wandering through the kitchen and the living room and the long hall, so crowded I had to weave through groups of people assessing me, touching my face, their arms around me, their voices in my ear. I was amazed that I was capable of speaking in a voice I recognized as my own.

At one point Professor Raab came over and introduced himself as

Steven's professor in constitutional law. He didn't mention the op-ed piece, but he asked about the flag. I told him I didn't know anything about the flag, and he didn't press me, filling the silence with talk of Steven as "remarkable," a "natural leader," "a person of integrity," things I imagined he had committed to memory on his drive to our house. He was an uncomfortable man.

My father said we were to say nothing about the flag or the op-ed piece and particularly we were not to mention the fact that Faith had been fired.

Faith glided through the room on her long, slender legs with ghostly grace, serving plates of chicken and pasta and baked fish and salad, speaking in confidential whispers to people who were strangers to her. I found the intimacy of her manner odd and wondered if she were as drunk as Milo was. By late afternoon Milo had slipped into a living room chair, falling in and out of sleep.

Only Bernard had the drawn face of long weeping.

"His stump hurts," Milo said crossly about Bernard's tears. I let the remark pass, because I knew that it wasn't Bernard's stump.

People never seemed to leave. They came and came at lunch and dinner and after dinner, into the night. Several visitors were still in the living room when my mother finally excused herself and went to her bedroom.

I followed her, sitting on the end of the bed watching her pace the room, her arms held tight across her chest.

"I'm angry," she said, as if the hysteria of the last hours had been spent and in its place came a hollow tunnel of sound. "I'm angry that Steven wrote the op-ed piece, but it was like him to write it, and he never would have imagined the price he'd finally pay for speaking out."

She lay down on the bed.

"We don't know why he was killed," I said feebly.

"We don't know and may never know, and how can I be angry at Steven for being himself, who I admired and loved beyond any life?" She turned the light on beside her bed, and in its glare her deep golden skin was painted with a thin green glaze.

"I want to kill the person who did it." She looked over at me dry-eyed. "It's normal, you understand. The way I feel is normal."

By two-thirty in the morning, the last of the visitors had gone. Faith was cleaning up the dishes, and Milo was dead asleep in the living room. From the kitchen window, I could see a light in the hangar and knew my father was there.

"David wants the door to Steven's room kept shut, Claire," Faith said wearily. "He asked me to tell you."

I drank the rest of a glass of red wine someone had left on the kitchen table.

"I wasn't planning on opening it," I said.

The light on my desk was on, not enough voltage to illuminate the room, and I stood watching the shapes in the room take form in the darkness. The rodents were complaining, the damaged bird chirped in weak captivity, everybody hungry, and I clapped my hands over my ears.

I lay on my side on the bed, my back to the window, my eyes closed, a film in my brain fast-forwarding from the table at the library with Steven to the moment rummaging in my backpack for the red umbrella and then to Steven's voice registering surprise and the image of him falling and falling.

I didn't want to feed the animals any longer.

I wanted them gone.

I got out of bed, tilted the lampshade on my desk in the direction of the cages, going first to the mouse cage with three fat gray field mice that in any case belonged outside. I should never have brought them in. I picked up the cage and walked over to the door, which led from my room to the yard, walked down the steps onto the small patch of grass, which remained between the house and the hangar, and dumped the mice in the grass.

The milk snake, a strange, mellow green color with diamonds on his back, had been a gift from my mother when I was studying reptiles as an undergraduate. He slid through my fingers, lacing himself in S's until I put him in the grass and he slithered away into the darkness.

Then I went to Olivia's cage. She was a small white rat I had rescued from the biology lab when the cancer with which she had been infected turned out not to be fatal. I went into the middle of the yard and set her down.

Back in my room, I put the empty cages in my closet.

Only the one-winged finch and the praying mantis remained.

From the top of my closet, I got some empty book boxes and packed the spider monkey skeleton and the caterpillar and the cobra's head, the kitten fetus lounging all these years in formaldehyde and the pallid bat my mother had brought home just yesterday morning. I put the boxes of treasures back on the shelf, closed the door and turned off my bedroom light.

Passing the large window on my way to the kitchen, my room dark, I could see Olivia shimmering white in the shaft of light coming from the hangar. She had moved farther away from the house—sitting on her haunches, her neck arched, looking around the new and dangerous world.

I shut the door to my bedroom, went through the kitchen, where Faith was just putting away the last of the pots, and opened the door to Steven's room.

"I'm sleeping here," I said, "in case my father asks you where I am."

THE LIFEGUARD CHAIR

Steven ordered dragonflies and damselflies for my twelfth birthday, and they were delivered as babies, many of them dead on arrival. In seventh-grade science, we were going to study metamorphosis and incomplete metamorphosis, and it was my job to watch the dragonflies grow up. They are examples of incomplete metamorphosis, which means they look the same when they're adults as they did as babies, only bigger. I knew this information from my biology book, but since most of my dragonflies were already dead, I arranged them on a clear glass plate and put them in the natural-history collection in my room.

What I love about the sanctuary I've assembled is its predictable order. It gives me pleasure to walk into my room knowing that everything will be exactly as I left it—the caterpillar on a blue silk cloth, the skeleton of a spider monkey, the fetus of a kitten in a jar of formaldehyde, the dried skin of a milk snake, a swallow reduced by time to feathers arranged in a fan on my bureau.

Now, after the arrival of Steven's birthday gift, I have a plate of leftover dragonflies.

I also have a living milk snake and a yellow finch and a few white mice. But I prefer my collection of the dead to the living creatures.

Change disturbs me. If I had been given a choice for changing from a baby to a grown-up, which I was not, I would have chosen without a doubt an incomplete metamorphosis over a complete one.

That way I would always be recognized as myself.

C.F., age 12

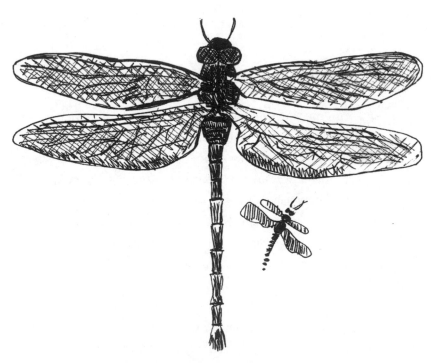

An example of incomplete metamorphosis

IV.

MAY 3: INCOMPLETE METAMORPHOSIS

I

On the morning of May 3, the day I met the man I would come to know as Victor Duarte—or V, as he asked me to call him—I returned to George Washington University for final exams. I had been at home living in Steven's room for a month.

April had been cold and wet. Dampness settled in the clothes and sheets and towels, crept deep into the bones. Even the kitchen with the stove on and filled with family felt subterranean.

The news of Steven's death went out on the UPI and AP wires, and there were stories all over the country, including several major ones and a long piece in the *New York Times Magazine* as well as a feature in the *Washington Post* titled "The Outsider," which quoted the dean of the law school as saying that Steven had "the lonely courage of the outsider."

My father refused to read the news stories, but I read them and so did Julia, collecting the clips from out of town, spread out on the coffee table in the living room for anyone to see.

" 'Lonely courage,' " Julia read aloud.

She was sitting at the kitchen table, where we all were in the first few days, picking at casseroles and sweets and roasted turkeys sent by friends, sticking close together.

"Decency never wins—don't you think that's true?" she said to no one in particular. "The losers are the courageous ones, in my opinion."

My father was sitting at the table, his chair angled toward a window that overlooked the hangar. For weeks he didn't initiate conversation, although he'd answer if one of us spoke to him.

" 'Lonely courage' is a good description of Steven, isn't it, David?"

"I don't think so," my father replied.

"Well, I like it, and so does Claire," my mother said, although I hadn't mentioned anything about the article. But I knew, and so did Julia, that Steven would have hated the word "courage" assigned to his name.

In the last weeks, I had turned into a skeleton draped with loose, transparent skin like silk. I was frightened all the time, sitting very still as if any movement could shatter my bones. I'd scrutinize my parents, examining them for cracks.

I began to notice that my father could no longer look at my mother. Even sitting next to her, he'd talk to a ghost of a person just beyond.

My mother wanted conversation. She'd sit on the edge of a ladder-back chair in the kitchen, lean into my father, her eyes locked on his face, her hand on his arm.

"Are you listening to me, David?" she'd ask.

"Of course, I am," he'd say, closing his eyes.

Feelings between them gathered in the dampness like mold.

In the lead of the first news story printed the second day after Steven was killed, Professor Raab was interviewed about the flag. "Just a coincidence," he was reported as saying. "Probably a prank, the work of some kids, perhaps. Someone in the neighborhood might have had a Justice Department flag."

My father supposed that neighbors, made significant by their proximity to our tragedy, could not keep themselves from speculating.

The op-ed piece was quoted, but the reporter, alerted by the FBI, said there was no evidence that Steven's death was related to that op-ed or any other he had written in the past. The story made no mention of Faith's termination from the Justice Department. Steven's death had overcome what happened to Faith, her firing a subject for silence in our family.

According to the reporter, Steven's death was more than likely a random killing, possibly accidental, unlikely political, too soon to speculate. There wasn't enough information to make a comment.

At the time of the shooting, there had been pandemonium. Students fled for safety into the buildings or rushed to Steven's aid, called for an ambulance and police, screamed, although I don't remember hearing anything.

There were no reliable witnesses as to the source of the gunshot, and though word went out on the radio and television stations, there was no trace of a gunman or a gun, no particular *reason* to conclude that Steven had been an intentional target.

The last major story about Steven's death, which wouldn't be written for some time, was the true one.

The FBI came often in the first week. They wanted us to give them lists of the people Steven knew, his present friends, old friends from elementary school and high school and university. Friends from the neighborhood. Anyone who might have taken issue with Steven. Anyone with an agenda, particularly people in authority who could hold a grudge.

We sat at the kitchen table making lists. We told the FBI about Faith and Charles Reed; about the dean of George Washington Law School, who had warned Steven to keep a low profile; about a friend of Steven's who was murdered in a hate killing for his homosexuality.

"What about your own friends?" they asked us. "Anyone among them who might take exception to Steven?"

We shook our heads.

"Trust your instincts," they said. "Instincts can be helpful to us."

Steven had had enemies, especially in high school, and I made a list of them. Julia brought up her suspicion that he might have belonged to a left-wing political organization that we didn't know about. My father remembered a serious run-in Steven had had with the principal of the junior high, who was later diagnosed with schizophrenia and hospitalized.

The FBI took an interest in that story.

They asked my father if any of his patients who'd died had families that might have had a reason to be angry.

"I lost a lot of patients when I was at NIH," he said. "It's a research institute, and we work primarily with the gravely ill."

"There was that boy of the woman who died of ALS the second year we lived here. Remember, David? It was right before you left NIH," Julia said.

"It was *why* I left NIH."

"You left because your patients didn't get better," Julia said. "That's what you always used to tell me."

"I left because they died," my father said.

"But the boy whose mother died wanted you to adopt him. I don't recall his name."

My father stiffened.

"Of course I couldn't adopt him," he said, defensive in a way I'd not ever seen him be—a wry, confident, interior man with an

occasional burst of temper. It was as though the FBI were questioning his humanity.

I gave them a list of Steven's girlfriends.

"Steven was always the one who broke up first," I said, a matter of
pride.

Julia remembered a particular boy at Walter Johnson High School
who kept losing in debate matches to Steven. At the last debate in se-
nior year, the boy lit a cherry bomb and threw it out the window of
the high school after the match.

"We need as many names as you can think of," the FBI said. "We'll
check these out and keep looking, and you keep remembering."

I had moved permanently to Steven's room after the FBI spent two
days going through his things, finding nothing of particular interest,
nothing private or suggestive, except love letters from various
women.

If I slept at all, I'd come to consciousness in a cold sweat. I was always afraid. For weeks I couldn't drive or leave the house or talk on
the telephone or read or sit at the kitchen table for dinner, and finally, by the end of the second week, I didn't leave Steven's room.

What I did was cut out pictures from my biology books. I cut out
a brightly colored glossy picture of a gossamer lacewing taking off in
flight from a leaf and taped it to the lampshade on Steven's desk. I
cut out a series of pictures from the section on incomplete metamorphosis describing the way a young insect ages by molting over and
over into adulthood.

On the wall beside Steven's desk, I tacked a photograph of the yellow striped Nomadidae bee, a species that assumes the defenses of a
yellow jacket although he has no stinger, and another color photograph of the nonstinging syrphid fly, which resembles a stinging

honeybee. I must have found some larval-stage defense system in these glossy pictures of benign species of insects imitating the appearance of stinging ones.

I developed simple routines to get through the day to darkness. A time for this and a time for that, so my calendar would have in its reliable pattern a satisfactory constancy, as long as I didn't leave Steven's bedroom.

At night I'd climb under the covers knowing I couldn't sleep and open what was left of my cut-up biology book to the section on metamorphosis, looking at a string of photographs—a caterpillar larva encased in a cocoon traveling from pupa to butterfly.

Metamorphosis was as close to a system of belief as any that I knew.

I tried not to think of Steven dead. But my mind would wander to his ashes in a celadon vase in the bookcase in my parents' bedroom.

Sometime, my mother told me, we'd scatter the ashes, and I believed that what remained of Steven's body would have the power to alter the landscape.

On my first day back at George Washington, Uncle Milo drove me to school.

"Milo can take you when he goes on his futile piano trip," my father said.

Milo was looking for a piano.

"There's no space in the living room for a piano," my father had said.

"I'm looking at uprights."

"There's no room for an upright."

"There is, David. I've measured. If we move the gray couch just a bit to the right toward the front door, there's room for a piano between the two windows facing south."

"I don't want a piano in the house," my father said.

"It's necessary," Milo said quietly. "I've come to believe that a piano is necessary."

We pulled up to the Gelman Library, and Milo stopped the car.

"Secondhand uprights. I check the newspaper," he said, touching my hand as I started to get out. "I'll pick you up at six tonight."

I pulled the sun visor down and checked the mirror.

"Do I look blue to you?" I asked.

"Why blue?"

"From lack of oxygen. When I leave the house, I have trouble breathing."

"Oh, Claire." He reached down and took my hand, surprising in Milo, who was awkward with intimacy.

But he had changed with Steven's death. He had responsibilities.

"You're not blue. Red or pink or whatever color a girl your age is supposed to be—that is the color you are."

2

My breath was high in my chest as I climbed out of the car, hardly enough air to go in the handicapped entrance to the library so I wouldn't have to see the steps where Steven had fallen. My plan—I was careful to fill the time I'd be away from Steven's room with arrangements so I wouldn't panic—was to go to the library until class. I'd spend no more than half an hour in the library going over my biology notes, then class, then my father's office so I could eat lunch in solitude, then lab, then a chemistry lecture and only half an hour before Milo would be back to pick me up.

The reading room where I always studied with Steven was half full, and I stood at the main door, checking to see if anyone familiar was there, not wishing yet to speak to someone I knew. Of my friends I had only been willing to see Eva.

I slipped off my jean jacket and hung it on a chair, opened my book bag, took out pencils and a notebook and my entomology text, aware that people at the long reading table were taking me into account.

A young woman with a bad cough was underlining in a book, which I recognized from Steven's bookcase as constitutional law. Maybe this woman had known him. Maybe she recognized me. There was a man in his early twenties, perhaps Egyptian or Ethiopian by the sharpness of his features, slouched in the chair, still in his coat and sleeping.

At the end of the table, Victor Duarte was sitting with a stack of books in front of him. Behind him a bank of windows facing east opened to a large vacant building in the process of being disassembled, and light from the dusty noonday sun fell across Victor's face, splitting it in half, spreading over the table where we were sitting.

Victor didn't look at me directly, but I could feel his attention.

He knows who I am, I thought, and he's curious about a young woman who has suffered violence and loss.

I moved my chair so it faced away from him, put my feet up on the next chair and rested a book in the bowl of my lap.

In a glance I had noticed things. That he was dark with strong features, large-boned, straight black hair long over the denim collar of his work shirt. Something surprising about him. I remember thinking at the time that it was his hands that caught my attention.

Perhaps the way he rested them on either side of the open book, his fingers broad and thick, crusted with dirt. Rough, working-class hands, not the hands of a student.

He leaned across the table

"I think I know who you are." His face was close to mine, and I drew back. "Claire Frayn?"

I nodded.

"I knew your brother."

My skin went suddenly clammy.

"I'm so very sorry," he said softly. "Such a terrible thing to happen!"

What I heard in the intensity of his voice—as if a lump were caught low in his throat—was the sound of grief.

"You knew him?"

"Steven was the person I wanted to be." He rested his chin on his fists. "I'm lucky he was my friend."

I didn't question what Victor said, not then and not for a long time, but I remembered it. Such a curious turn of sentence, and I must have had an odd expression on my face, because he shook his head.

"What I mean to say is, Steven and I had common interests," he said.

"In law school, you met him?" I asked.

"I'm not in law school," he said, leaning back in his chair. "I'm an engineer."

I noticed every detail that morning, not just about Victor Duarte but everything, my first time in public since Steven's death, charting a new geography.

I must have seemed anxious, because he touched my arm, just a glance, a sympathetic gesture, but I pulled away.

"If you'd ever like to talk with someone about your brother," he said, "call me." He scribbled down his number. "Only if you'd like." His manner was almost apologetic.

I hadn't been aware of wanting anything since Steven died, as if, like the kitten on my bureau, I was preserved in a state of stillness.

Something in the way Victor had spoken to me, the surprise of his friendship with Steven, the promise of information about my brother, provoked me.

"I don't want to push you to talk, but I knew your brother well," he said.

"How well?" I asked, my defenses at risk.

"We saw each other often, nearly every day, including the afternoon he died."

He pushed the slip of paper with his telephone number on it across the table.

In biology lecture I kept my eyes on the clock over the lectern—one of those clocks with a minute hand that jumped three minutes at a time. The lecture hall was full, so I sat in the back, my head down, taking notes for what seemed hours and hours, until finally the class was over and I hoisted the heavy book bag on my shoulder, leaving first before anyone else, before the professor had reassembled his notes, heading out the swinging door and down the corridor toward my father's office.

A young woman I'd never seen before, with red hair and tiny feet the size of a child's, was seated in my father's chair, leaning over papers spread out on the table he used as a desk, drinking a Diet Pepsi from a can. Something my father would never do at this desk, which had belonged to his grandfather.

The desk was cherry, made by his grandfather for the kitchen of the family's cottage in Llangollen, North Wales, and was my father's only treasure besides his airplane.

I wanted to tell the woman to pick up her papers and her Diet Pepsi before she ruined the wood.

A small transgression by Dr. Delores Lucas, a resident in infectious diseases substitute teaching my father's classes for the semester, I discovered later.

But I was enraged just at the sight of her infringing on our lives— a careless, red-haired girl with tiny feet, one high-heeled strappy shoe kicked off like an insult to the Frayn family, lying on its side on the brightly colored Welsh rug.

In the pocket of my trousers was the torn piece of paper with

Victor Duarte's telephone number. I walked to the end of the corridor, slipped into a telephone booth, dropped two quarters in the slot and dialed.

"I'm calling for Victor Duarte," I said to the man who answered the phone, my heart thumping in my chest so hard it almost felt visible through my red T-shirt, thin as I was.

There was reason for me to be nervous, but at that moment, perhaps in my innocence or even arrogance, I believed that I *understood* Victor Duarte, the way a person does who has some knowledge of chemical properties, a science student or a cook or even a young woman like me, who believed, as I then did, that I had a particular gift of intuition and that, with my training in life sciences, I could imagine the life of a stranger from a single detail.

In the case of Victor Duarte, the secret was in his hands.

"This is Victor," he said.

"I'm Steven Frayn's sister," I said.

"Oh, hello."

Just the absence of a personal greeting disarmed me. Maybe he had forgotten my name. Maybe I was of no importance to him except as a recipient of news about Steven.

"You suggested I call."

"I'm glad you have."

He must have been smoking, because I heard a slow intake of breath.

"I'd very much like to have a conversation with you about your brother." He hesitated. There was something compelling and comforting in his voice, its low, gravelly tone, its measured calm.

"I want you to know that I admired Steven beyond words," he said.

I pressed the receiver close to my ear.

"I've been thinking you'd probably like to know about me, since

I'm a stranger and you have a right to feel threatened by strangers, especially now," he said, the formal precision of his speech familiar, reminding me of my father.

"I'm a civil engineer with an interest in law and ethics, which is why I sometimes take my lunch hour to study in the library."

He spoke in a whisper as if the information were classified.

"I'm single, and I live just south of Union Station with my sister, Isabel, who's three years younger than me," he said. "The same age difference between you and Steven."

It was a small detail, the kind that suggests a keen ear, a capacity for intimacy, and I took note, making something of it, a close friendship with my brother, grounds for trust.

Victor Duarte was cunning. I'm sure he knew what he was doing, but a year ago last May I knew nothing of the subtle intricacies of relationships.

And so we agreed to meet in a small café called Café Rouge on the edge of the campus after my last class of the day.

3

I arrived early. I'd never been to this café at Twenty-second and G in the middle of the university campus, although I'd often walked down the street on my way to meet Eva at Daisy's Coffee and Sweets. But this place I'd never noticed, a slip in the wall between two buildings, nothing to define it except for a dark red door, CAFÉ ROUGE written in purple letters across the top.

Victor Duarte must have chosen the place for its darkness. I could barely see my way across the crowded room, with its polished wooden tables and booths lit by low-wattage lamps with green glass shades hanging over the middle of the tables.

I chose a booth in the corner, self-consciously alone, checking the room to see if I'd been noticed. I pulled out the menu that was stuck behind the salt and pepper, holding it under the dim light. A limited menu, handwritten—sandwiches, fried fish, chili, beer, wine, coffee. A cover charge at night for live music. I could barely see the clientele, although I judged from the muted, earnest conversations that they were mainly graduate students. Probably older students came to this café, which was why I didn't know of it—degree candidates in business and law, working students who went to school at night, students who had careers.

When Victor Duarte slipped into the seat across from me, I was flipping through the pages of my entomology text.

He had changed clothes, wearing jeans and a starched red shirt with the sleeves rolled up, a bandanna around his head, his face damp with perspiration, although the weather that afternoon was cool. He had on old work boots full of caked mud, which I didn't notice until later, when he walked out of the café in front of me.

"I've never been here," I said, my mouth dry with nerves, the words sticking to my tongue.

"I'm not surprised."

He ordered a beer and a bag of pretzels and reached into his back pocket for two folded newspapers that he put on the table.

"You?" he asked.

"Just coffee."

"Regular students don't come here, which is why you're not aware of it," he said.

"Who does?"

An expression of amusement slid across his eyes, as if he were remembering a private joke. Something I'd see in his face again and again in the next month.

"For a long time, ever since Martin Luther King was killed— Were you even alive then?" He smiled at me, and probably I blushed.

"I wasn't."

"Nor was I, but I know that since the riots in Washington after his death, Café Rouge has been a political meeting place for all kinds of people with a gripe about the state of affairs—occasionally students, but mainly the underclass, working class, immigrants."

He opened the pretzels, dumping them on the table, pushing some in my direction.

"Help yourself."

He looked up, and I noticed he had a deep dimple in his chin and that his eyes in the dim green light were flat, too black for me to see the pupils.

For no reason I could name—my own peculiar dread, a vague notion of danger, caffeine I shouldn't have ordered, I was trembling.

"Where did you meet Steven?" I asked, trying to keep my voice from rising.

"Here," Victor said. "I met him over a year ago in the winter." He indicated a long, crowded table across the room, mostly men, one woman, her back to me, with steel-gray hair to her waist.

"I was sitting at that table with my buddies, like Rosie over there with the gray hair, and we were having a beer together when your brother walked into the café alone."

He rested his heavy arm next to my folded hands.

"How did you know it was Steven?" I asked.

"I recognized him from the newspaper."

He picked up one of the articles he'd taken out of his pocket, unfolded it and put it down on the table between us.

"Check out that photograph."

I held the newspaper up just under the light. There was a grainy picture I recognized from the front page of the Metro section, taken the previous October. It was a group photograph that my mother had clipped and framed, propping it among the photographs of strangers in the living room. Three young men and a woman. It had been taken at a vigil for a young George Washington University law student from Trinidad killed in an attack on homosexuals at a bar on P Street. Steven, identified as "outspoken law-student leader Steven Frayn," had spoken at the vigil. The woman standing next to him, the only other person named in the photograph, was Anna See, his girlfriend at the time.

He folded the newspaper and put it back in his pocket.

"I knew it was Steven when he came in the café because I'd saved the newspaper, and when I saw him, I put two and two together."

"He never told me anything about you."

"Steven was a man of secrets."

"Not with us," I said quickly, ashamed to fall upon information about my brother from a stranger.

"We're a close family." I was defensive. "Steven probably told you that."

"I sensed from things he said."

"We all live together, sort of on top of each other in the same little house." The words came toppling out. "Even my aunt and uncle and cousin. We're that close."

"You're very lucky," he said. "It's rare to have a close family anymore."

"Maybe." I was tentative.

Were we that close? We thought of ourselves as an island pitched in the middle of the sea, but perhaps such thinking was illusion or desperate hope; perhaps we were only our own story of a close family. My father in his hangar, me in my sanctuary for the dead, and Julia. Poor Julia. I had a rush of feeling for my mother, with her photographs of strangers framed among the pictures of us, as if there were never enough company in her house.

Rubbing my hands, which were damp with nerves, my eyes wandering as if I were in the process of a neurological event, I tried to concentrate on Victor's face.

"Did Steven mention that we live very quietly?" I asked. "We're not political."

I could feel the ground shifting, the way it does at the edge of the water when the waves come in and drag the sand back with them. Going under is how it felt, the water over my head.

"How can I explain?" He spoke slowly, his brow furrowed, as though he wanted to be sure I understood the exact nature of what he was saying, that he didn't mislead me or let out the wrong truth by accident. "I'm part of a group called DTT which stands for Demand Tolerance Today. Steven didn't belong, but we thought of him as a kind of heroic figure, sympathetic to our point of view, with the courage to speak out."

My chest tightened, the air trapped in my throat.

So Julia had been right about Steven.

"He never told me anything about your group," I said.

"He wouldn't have mentioned us," he said. "We don't advertise ourselves."

I looked away, unable to meet his steady gaze, feeling a little sick from too much coffee or excitement or fear.

"You don't have to believe me," he said. "I can't give you proof, but I'm going to ask for your help."

He was breaking up the pretzels into small pieces with a kind of nervous fastidiousness, ordering them in stacks lined up exactly. In the light over the table, I could see black dirt in the lines of his hands, marked by work.

"Steven talked about you."

He ran his hands through his hair—hands, I noticed, in constant motion, palm to palm, folded in a grip, pulling at his chin as if he had a beard.

"Steven told me you're a biologist."

"He told you that?"

"Well, you are, aren't you?"

I flushed. "A biology student," I said. "Not a biologist yet."

"But you will be." Victor checked his watch, rubbed it against his shirt and checked again. "It's getting late, and I've got something going on tonight."

"Six o'clock, and my uncle is picking me up soon."

"Then I'll hurry. I have something else from the newspaper to show you."

He unfolded a page from the *Washington Post*, the print smudged and faded.

"November fourteenth last year," he said, flattening the newspaper on the table, pushing it across to me. "Check the third page of the first section, bottom of the fold." He pressed his broad thumb on a photograph. "This photograph."

The picture was of two men and the shadow of a third. I squinted to read the caption under it.

The older man in the photograph was Charles Reed just after his swearing in as an assistant attorney general of the United States. He was standing with his son, Benjamin, a graduate student in musical composition at the University of Michigan. In the right-hand corner, his back to the camera, was the president of the United States.

I pushed the page across the table, my mind racing. Did Victor Duarte know about us? Had Steven told him personal stories, and had he heard that Charles Reed had fired my aunt Faith on the day that Steven died? Did he know about the Justice Department flag?

"Are you asking do I *know* these people?" I said.

"You know who Charles Reed is," he said. "Your aunt worked for him."

"How did you know that?"

"From Steven, and now the story's gotten around." His face was too close to mine. I could feel his breath, my own breath trapped in my throat.

"You must have read the op-ed piece that Steven wrote about the Civil Rights Division of the Justice Department," I said.

"He showed the piece to me the night he died."

He folded the paper and put it back in his pocket, looking just past me as if at something behind my head.

"Something else," he began, clearing his throat. "I've reason to think that Benjamin Reed might have had some role in your brother's death."

I pressed my fingers hard against my mouth until my lips went numb.

"We have been suspicious of Benjamin for a while."

I heard his voice at a distance, as if he were speaking from across the room, and I had to strain to hear him, in spite of a crushing pressure on my chest.

" 'We' is the DTT. The same group I mentioned to you. I knew Benjamin, not well, but I knew him in elementary school."

I checked my hands to see if they were shaking, and they were, and my throat was closing, the air too thin in the café. I wanted to go home.

"I think I smell smoke," I said.

"Cigarettes," he said.

"It smells like something's burning."

"Nothing's burning," he said. "You're probably nervous. I would be in your place."

"We don't talk about politics in my family," I said, as if politics were the subject of our conversation. My head resting against the wall was such a weight, as if, unhinged, it might drop off. "We never talk about politics. Even after Steven was killed and we had to wonder—"

"You must understand that I'm not saying Benjamin Reed was *the* one. Just that he might know something."

He got up from the booth, pulled a chair over to the end of the table so he could sit closer to me, speaking quietly. "Once, at this café, Steven and I were having a beer, and your name came up, and he spoke about you with real sweetness. 'A true believer,' is what he said of you. I knew I'd be pleased to meet you sometime. Not like this, but sometime."

I looked down at the shiny wood table, memorizing its grain.

"What I'd like from you—and this is what I mean by help, and please know you're a free agent and ought to come to your own decision—but I'd like to meet Benjamin Reed. I'd like to have a chance to talk to him."

"I don't understand what you're asking me to do."

He tipped his chair back, and at that angle, a shadow falling across one side of his face, his expression disturbed me. I felt vaguely ill.

"I was thinking you could begin a correspondence with him— with Benjamin Reed—and when he comes back to Washington in the summer to visit his father, which I'm sure he'll do, you can arrange to meet him, and we'll find an opportunity for you to introduce him to me."

He folded his arms behind his head casually, as if we were having an easy conversation about nothing at all.

"I have no reason to write a stranger," I said.

"You'd invent a reason," he said. "Anything. You can say anything to engage his interest. But you can't be yourself of course—not Claire Frayn. He'd figure that out in a second."

Now, in the present time, I can't for the life of me re-create the texture of that moment except as fact. My hands were clasped, my fingers gripped to stop the shaking. Victor Duarte reached over, unfolded my hands, flattened the palms down on the table and put his own hands on top of mine, pressing them into the wood until the tension broke and the trembling stopped and I found myself like a sleepwalker acquiescing to his plan.

I suppose it also made a kind of sense to me that all the pieces of the story of what happened on the day of Steven's murder—the Justice Department flag, Charles Reed and Faith and the op-ed about the Civil Rights Division of the Justice Department—could fall together and include Charles Reed's son.

"If this Benjamin does know what happened to Steven, why would he tell you?" I asked.

"People do strange things." Victor stood to leave. "In elementary school Benjamin was cruel to the nobodies, guys like me. He'd get people to gang up, and he had a bad temper."

I checked the clock over the bar. Six-ten. Milo would be waiting, and I wanted to see him, to rush to the car and climb in the front seat and listen to my uncle whine and complain, jabbering in his familiar way about upright pianos.

"I have to go now," I said, slinging my book bag over my shoulder.

"Don't worry. There's plenty of time for you to decide to do something about this or not." He reached into his pocket to pay. "Make little of what I've asked, Claire. It's just a suggestion, a possibility."

I followed him out of the café, far enough behind that I could see the dried mud dropping from his work boots, leaving a trail of dark red dust.

4

Milo was waiting at Twenty-first and H, drumming on the steering wheel, when I climbed into the front seat, closed the door and leaned back against the headrest.

"Fasten your seat belt," he said.

I pulled the strap across my chest, sinking into the seat, closing my eyes.

"Now you're yellow." Milo reached across to touch my face.

"When I let you off today, you thought you were turning blue, and instead you've turned this bronzy yellow, almost golden."

"Yellow?" I didn't open my eyes.

Milo laughed. "It's the light from the setting sun falling across your lovely face, turning you yellow. Golden yellow. Very nice."

He pulled out of the parking place and turned on H, headed to Twentieth and home.

"I'm playing Schubert's *Trout*. Can you hear it? Just the melody. Dee-dum, dee-dum, dee-dum. Like that."

"I saw you were playing the steering wheel," I said, hoping my voice didn't sound as shaky to Milo as it did to me.

My body gave in to a powerful exhaustion, relieved to be in the closed car, headed home, the sun sinking quickly behind us, relieved to be hidden by the coming dusk so Milo couldn't examine the color of my face anymore.

"I'd really like to get a baby grand. The sound is so much better," Milo was saying. "Or maybe rent one, but it would stick out in the middle of the living room and block the window, so I have found an upright on sale."

I was too distracted by my meeting with Victor Duarte for conversation.

"Did you hear me?"

I nodded.

"So I bought it. I bought a Rangely upright, one-third off, and it will fit right in between the windows in the living room next to the couch. You know where I mean?"

"I think I do."

"It should be delivered Friday."

I could tell without opening my eyes we were going around Sheridan Circle, the way I was flung against the door. Milo wasn't good at negotiating circles.

Every time I drove around Sheridan Circle with Julia on our way downtown, she reminded me that a car bomb had exploded there, killing some important Latin Americans, maybe Chilean, maybe Argentinean—she didn't know, and she didn't remember why they were important, but their deaths had to do with the CIA. Although it happened a long time before we even moved to Washington, my mother dealt with all historical disasters as current events.

"Do you know *why* the piano was on sale?" Milo was asking.

"I don't."

"The salesman told me pianos aren't selling. No one wants music at home. Just the radio and CDs, but nothing that takes up a lot of room like a piano. No one to play the piano, is what the salesman said. Are you listening?"

"I'm listening," I said.

"This is important. He said to me, this salesman who sold me the Rangely upright, said that it all started with 9/11 and then the war in Iraq, but ever since Steven Frayn died—he didn't remember Steven's name, of course, but he said ever since that law student at George Washington University was killed, the city has gotten worse, more and more dangerous, uneasiness everywhere. People are no longer interested in pianos."

"Did you tell the piano salesman you're related to the law student?"

"I told him nothing at all. My only conversation was about pianos, and when he mentioned Steven, I decided to purchase the piano quickly just to divert his attention."

"Good, Milo. We don't need everyone to know who we are."

"But they *do* know," Milo said. "It was as if I were transparent and he could see things about me I hadn't told him—just an ordinary piano salesman with X-ray eyes. When he mentioned Steven, I may have turned bone white, but I promise you I didn't say a word. And, Claire?"

"Yes?"

"Don't tell Julia about the piano yet."

"I promise I won't," I said.

"I'll play a lot of Mozart. Cheerful stuff. Your father likes cheerful, and he'll get used to it, and pretty soon, maybe even weeks from now, the piano will have done its work and your father will be better. I assure you of that. We'll all be better."

"I hope."

"Hope is good," Milo said.

When we arrived home, the candles were lit, a thick veal stew in a pot in the middle of the table, wine already open. Everyone was sitting around the kitchen table, including Lisha, who ate with us often.

"You're late, Milo." Julia was serving the plates. "If you're late because you bought a piano, don't tell David."

My father wasn't at the table. The lights were on in the hangar, and he was working on the left wing of the plane that had been his obsession for the last month. He seldom came to dinner. After we'd eaten, after the dishes were done and we'd all disappeared to our own rooms, me to Steven's, he would come into the house and finish off what was in the pots my mother had left simmering on the stove for him.

"I have a migraine and may not be able to make it through dinner," Julia said, handing Milo a bottle of wine to pass.

Julia blamed herself.

"I shouldn't have had so many opinions," she said. "That's where Steven got it."

No one disagreed.

When Steven was young, she had been amused by his strong

temperament, proud when people remarked that for a little boy Steven certainly had a lot to say for himself. When his opinions got him attention, especially bad attention, she told Steven that she admired him, admired that he took a position, put himself on the line. "You're afraid of nothing," she'd tell him, thrilled to have a "front man" in the house, since my father meandered the paths of theoretical thinking, skirting the difficult decisions. Steven was her kindred spirit.

"I was wrong," she'd say. "I should have taught him consequences."

I sat down in the seat next to Bernard, keeping myself at a distance. Bernard had developed an odd condition, perhaps of the esophagus, so he seemed to be choking even when he wasn't eating, an occasional gurgling in his throat as if at any moment something would bubble over.

"Do you mind stopping that noise, Bernard?" Julia asked, passing him a plate of stew.

"It's involuntary, Aunt Julia."

Faith laid her hand on Bernard's arm. "Try, darling," she said quietly. "I believe you can stop it."

"David's working on the plane," Milo said, stating the obvious to change the subject. "I saw him when we came in." He poured wine for himself and for me and passed the bottle around the table.

"None for me," Faith said.

"Then I'm going to drink your share, too," Milo said, drinking his own glass quickly.

"Don't," Julia said. "There's too much disorder in this house for anyone to become an alcoholic."

"You're not my mother, Julia," Milo said, filling his glass to the rim. "A pity, but a fact."

"I'm not anybody's mother any longer," Julia said, getting up from the table, opening the door to the garden, heading to the hangar.

"She can't help it," Bernard said when Julia had left.

"She *can* help it," Faith said. "Poor Lisha. Dinner here can't be good for you."

"We're all having a hard time," Lisha said. "I may as well be here having a hard time than at home, where my parents want me to look on the bright side."

"What does that mean?" Milo asked.

"They're parents. They hate to see me unhappy."

"Maybe you'll meet someone," Bernard said, and, sensing the silence in the room, he added, "Maybe I shouldn't have said that."

"Maybe not," I said.

I waited until I saw my mother leave the hangar to walk around to the front of the house, and then I left the table.

My father had his back to me when I came in, leaning against the right wing of the plane, one ankle crossed over the other, his left hand in his pocket, staring at something just ahead.

"Hello," I said.

He had moved a couple of plastic chairs into the hangar, and I sat down on one of them.

"Hello, darling."

He had a lovely way of saying "darling," low in his throat, dropping the g, making a song of the word, as if "darling" were reserved for me alone.

"How was your first day back?"

"All right." I rearranged myself, tucked my legs under me, pulled my jacket closed. The hangar was always cold.

"I was thinking," he began, taking a cigarette out of his jacket pocket without lighting it, sitting across from me. "That's what I was doing when you came in. Thinking I'm not the person I thought I was."

"You actually had time to think with Julia here?" I asked.

"I thought right through her conversation. It's one of my very few accomplishments."

We both laughed. We could still do that together, and I was relieved.

He had been frozen with sadness. Every movement of his long body seemed final, as if he were in the slow process of disintegrating. He seldom spoke in the company of the whole family.

This was my first visit to the hangar since Steven had died, and I was surprised to see that in the far corner, the back side of the garden, my father had moved his office from their bedroom. There were his books and his computer, a figure of a naked woman about a foot tall with flexible parts, which his father had given him when he left Wales to come to the United States for medical school.

He lit the cigarette and looked up at me, giving my foot a gentle kick.

"You've moved your office," I said.

"It was too crowded in the bedroom. I couldn't think, and besides, Milo is looking for a piano to cheer me up. Who needs that additional noise."

It was a statement.

I loved my father's angular face, the thin, unkempt white hair and long legs, which he crossed at the knee in a European way. "Room temperature" was my mother's description of his cool restraint, but I could imagine a tempest hidden in the recesses of his brain, virgin passions like mine, a girl in love with dead creatures.

"You've got something on your mind," he said.

I was tentative.

I had come to him about Victor Duarte, but I didn't know what to ask in order to get the answer I wanted to hear. Not any answer would do and I wanted no questions from him either. What I wanted from my father was permission.

Something had happened to me with Victor. It was almost a metabolic change, as if I'd been ill for a very long time, sick almost to death, and as I left the Café Rouge, the illness seemed to float out of me. An unexpected burst of energy, an intimation of health.

What Victor had given me was an enemy. I *wanted* to believe that Benjamin Reed had killed Steven. A flesh-and-blood enemy, and my desire for revenge was so powerful that I put out of mind a reasonable doubt.

It's difficult now for me to understand how I, training to be a scientist with hours of laboratory observations, could possibly have latched so quickly on to Victor's story, but I've learned that in a state of fear I'm capable of anything, including dying.

"Julia thinks that what Steven wrote in the op-ed piece could have been interpreted as an actual threat to the government," was how I began my conversation with my father, taking a roundabout route. I wanted to ask him about Steven and the government, particularly the Justice Department, and in a backhanded way about Victor Duarte.

"Do you think Julia's right?"

"That's her political hysteria," he said. "The government wouldn't bother with one young law student writing op-ed pieces. It's not in the business of killing its citizens, if that's what you're implying."

He leaned back and stretched his legs, looking out the Plexiglas window of the hangar into darkness.

"I guess that's what I'm implying," I said.

"This is a democracy, different than the one I grew up with, but a democracy nevertheless," he said. "In Wales we have an adversary, and that's England, but we can't do anything about England except complain. I like knowing the enemy." He flicked his ashes on the ground and rubbed them into the cement. "I don't know an enemy here. Except fear. Fear could be it."

"I've been afraid since Steven died," I said.

"I suppose I am, too," he said. "Sick with it."

"I was never afraid until he was killed, and since then I'm frightened all the time," I said. "Until today. Today I feel a little different."

I was hoping he would tell me to trust my own judgment. And if he had asked me at that moment about my meeting with Victor, if he had asked me any questions at all, I might have told him what had happened at Café Rouge and this story as it developed might have been a different one. Or not.

I know now I was at an intersection, balancing between a permanent and familiar girlhood and something else. A misty state of mind in the process of resolving to a kind of clarity. I doubt that anything my father could have said would have made a difference in what I chose to do. As Faith used to say during family arguments in the kitchen, "choice" is just another word for destiny.

My father's computer was open to a medical chat room, and he turned it off, straightened some papers, reached into a cup and handed me a chocolate kiss wrapped in silver paper.

"Are you working?" I asked.

"On the airplane," he said. "Nothing else. I just open the computer so the screen is full."

He moved a book away from the edge of his desk, and my eyes followed his hand, not to the book, which was one of his technical science texts, but to a photograph propped up beside it, leaning against a pencil holder full of pencils.

The photograph was of a young woman I had never seen, with dark hair in a floppy bun piled on the top of her head, high cheekbones, deep hooded black eyes, a dimple on one side of her small mouth.

"Who is that?"

He had caught my line of vision. "A girl from my school in Wales."

"I've never heard you mention her."

"Her name was Meryn Thomas." He squinted, looking at the picture. "I've put her photograph up because she's dead," he said, as if this explanation made perfect sense. "If that's what you were wondering."

"I wasn't wondering," I said, uneasy in such close proximity to my father's inner life.

Too quickly, I got up from the chair and crossed the hangar, passing over a shadow of the half-finished airplane cast by the fluorescent light on the dirt floor where I was walking.

"The girl in the photograph was eighteen, going off to study voice with the Welsh National Opera," he began as I moved to open the door to the hangar. "And then, in the winter before she left, we were skating on the frozen river Dee, and she died."

"How?" I asked.

"She fell through the ice."

I was a small plane's length away from him, and when I turned around, he had taken the photograph off his desk and put it in his lap.

"That was why I left Wales and came here to study medicine," he said.

"I didn't know that," I said.

Of course I didn't know it. He had never told me, and I knew now that he wanted something of me he couldn't request, sympathy or information or a question about this girl so he could tell me what had happened. It slipped through and out of my mind, then and other times in the months ahead, but I knew I'd heard this story before, or something like it. I didn't put it together with the boy whose mother died at NIH until much later.

I suppose I had come to the hangar with something to tell him about Victor, discovering instead that he had his own secret.

So I turned away and opened the door to the garden without looking back.

5

When I glanced through the picture window in the kitchen, Milo was leaning over the table speaking to Bernard, Faith was doing the dishes, and my mother, on her way to the bedroom, her blouse already unbuttoned to change for bed, was saying something in Faith's ear. Lisha must have left while I was in the hangar.

Just seeing my family framed by the window, I wanted to disappear.

I walked out the gate, past our house, past the Denvers' across the street, their old poodle sitting in the house on the back of the couch barking at nothing, past the Paillons', their curtains drawn, Madame Paillon in a second-floor window in her robe although it wasn't even nine o'clock. I hurried past the Hsus, since Dr. Hsu had just opened the front door, saying something quite loud but in Mandarin to his bad tempered German shepherd. Our neighborhood was full of dogs, mostly large ones, and there was supposed to be a leash law, which was observed by the foreign scientists, but the Americans tended to let their dogs run free in spite of complaints. I was leery of Dr. Hsu's shepherd, since the doctor was too small a man to control a large dog with an agenda, so I hurried up Newland Street, turning left at Fairway.

It was cold for May, with water in the air thick enough to dampen my face, an English evening, and the freshness of it cleared my mind. I had an odd, disembodied feeling of floating just off the ground, like a seaplane skimming the water, a lightness to my footsteps. No tracks.

Fairway Street was almost completely dark. Only two streetlights at the end of the road as far as I could see, and the houses were char-coal shadows against a line of bushy trees. Except the first house, which belonged to the Banks with slivers of light coming through the shutters and the porch light on, so I could see the artificial blue wreath the Banks put up sometime around Christmas and forgot to take down for months. Their garbage had been put out on the road for Wednesday's collection, and I heard something rummaging around in the trash—a raccoon, possibly a rat or a possum. We had all three in the neighborhood, though not nearly as many rats as the city, but lately I'd developed a fear of animals, even domestic ones, so I crossed the street, which without the light from the Banks' porch was absolutely black.

I seldom walked in the neighborhood and never at night, so until this moment I wasn't aware that I could be afraid of the dark. An ef-fort had been made in these suburbs to create the illusion of rural safety, the properties on half acre lots with long front yards running to the street—no sidewalks—very few streetlights, an occasional view at night into the lives of people willing to keep their blinds open. A menacing loneliness, as if some of the houses had been closed down.

We knew the names of the neighbors, most of them visiting scien-tists at NIH. Julia had parties for the neighbors, usually in the sum-mer, but the houses were always changing occupants, scientists coming and going, living at a remove, suspicious of strangers, iso-lated in the airtight shoe boxes of our suburban neighborhood.

At night in the part of the city I knew, around the university, it was noisy and full of light, and I was always in the company of someone, so I'd never felt this particular chill along my spine before.

I was walking with some haste, thinking about Victor Duarte, filled with a sense that someone could be following—even Dr. Hsu's German shepherd, broken free of its leash.

I used to think I had the mind of a dancer with a dancer's eye for spacial parameters, or maybe the mind of an athlete or an animal, not particularly complex, with minimal defenses, relying on an instinct for the moment.

And in that moment, walking through my childhood neighborhood in the dark, sufficiently alert to what was around me, I *knew* I had already made a decision that Victor Duarte was central to my life.

A light rain had started to fall, and my hair was wet, my head chilly. At the end of Fairway, I turned left again, planning to head around the block. One more left turn and I'd be back at Newland, two houses from home. But I didn't know the neighborhood except for my block, although I'd lived there almost all my life. I used to walk to elementary school, but that walk took me through my backyard onto Ames Drive, and in high school I drove with Steven first and then with Eva, paying little attention to these interior roads. Now when I left the house to go to school or to Eva's or another friend's or downtown, I drove straight out of the subdivision to River Road and back the same way.

I decided I would call Victor as soon as I got home. Just call. Wait for him to answer, hear his voice, a kind of reality check, and then I'd hang up without speaking. I had nothing *yet* to say to him.

What I had was an enemy.

I said his name over and over into the wet air, where it dissolved without an echo, lost in the damp sponge of night. *Benjamin, Benjamin Reed.* Just repeating his name, I saw his bony face in the newspaper photograph, the spill of black hair across his forehead, the deceptive formality of his posture.

A man capable of killing my brother.

I felt my mind and body organize to the possibility of an enemy. It was like learning to walk again, or for the first time, an initial uncertainty and then one foot in front of the other and again and again, until it became almost easy and familiar, as the body moves forward in a certain direction.

Which is how it was that night, walking along in the darkness, an occasional slip on the black road, falling only once, and then just on my knee. I lost track of time and where I was and whether I'd passed the next left I was supposed to take home or whether I'd walked beyond it. But there would be another turn, I thought, and in any case I had a purpose, a place to put my grief to use.

Already a letter to Benjamin Reed, the murderer, was forming itself in my mind.

Dear Mr. Reed.

No. That was wrong. Too formal.

Dear Benjamin Reed,

You don't know me, but I have seen you on occasion and most recently in person when I was at the Justice Department picking up a letter for my mother from a friend. I think it was you I saw on the elevator. But I did see the newspaper photograph of you and your father and thought when I saw it—"THERE he is!"

Because—and this is what I write to tell you—my brother died a year ago last February 15 of encephalitis, and when I saw you and then later in the newspaper photograph, I lost my breath, because you look exactly like him. Exactly. You could be the same person. Even the way your hair falls across your forehead.

So I'm hoping to have a correspondence with you, and perhaps when you are home for your summer holiday, we can meet.

I am twenty-three and finished university and am presently working in musical composition, as my dream is be a composer. I play the piano well enough. Quite well, I suppose. We have an up-right. It's what we can afford.

I'm the second-eldest of six children, counting my dead brother, Alberto, who was the first child in a conservative Catholic family. My aunt Louella works for the Justice Department. So, you see, we have things in common, even a background in South America.

In the hope of becoming your friend, Sophia Lupe
　Sophia Lupe.

Out of the blue, the name came, like the lyrics to an old song I had forgotten but used to sing.

Until that evening spent walking alone along a dark suburban road, a scientist by training, concerned with the observation of minute detail, I had no idea of the hairpin turns my imagination was capable of making.

At some point I began to realize that I was lost. I had taken three—or was it four or maybe even five?—left turns, and it must have gotten to be quite late.

I stopped to lean against a tree and listen. In the darkness, just along the road from the tree where I was standing, a house began to materialize, a long, one-story ranch house like ours was, with a light around the side, perhaps only a small night-light, so little brightness came of it. Somewhere I heard a voice. A sound that repeated and re-peated until I began to hear my name—*Claire! Claire!*—traveling the space between somewhere and the tree where I was leaning.

But it wasn't my name I heard. Just something I turned into the sound of *Claire* because I was lost.

I slid down the tree, sitting on the heavy roots, a little damp, wet-ting my trousers but not particularly cold, not too cold for me to wait for someone to come, for lights to go on in the ranch house across the street, even for daylight.

Maybe I fell asleep, I'm not certain, but suddenly I did hear *CLAIRE,* and the familiar voice was my mother's.

"What did you think you were doing going out alone in the dark for a walk in the middle of the night? Something you've *never* done?"

I climbed into the passenger seat, drew my knees up and rested my chin on them.

"Walking," I said.

"You don't *like* to walk. You told me that yourself. You said walking bored you when I suggested you take walks to ease the sadness, and so in the middle of the night—"

"I left no later than nine o'clock."

"—you go out for a walk in a neighborhood where a stranger can put a stolen flag on our front porch the day before he kills your brother."

"You don't know that."

"*Someone* killed your brother. It's not a safe place to walk here."

My mother was in the pajamas she sometimes wore—a kind of fetching combination of sexuality and nonsense—red silk pajamas with a huge white hibiscus print, and spread all over her face like a milk-white mask was the thick cream Europeans used for their babies' bottoms.

"I was lost," I said. "I would have been back sooner."

"Of course you were lost," she said. "This neighborhood is a maze. I want to move."

"Thank you for coming to find me."

"Of course I'd come find you," she said, winding through the dark streets, turning in to Newport.

I had been so close to home, little more than a block away, but I hadn't a sense of it at all, as if when I was young I had missed learning the territory of my childhood altogether, thinking my own street went on and on into infinity.

"You believed I'd go to bed—ho hum—and fall into one of those lovely, dreamless sleeps thinking nothing of my dead son or missing daughter, as if they'd been a blip on my march to old age."

"Shut up, Mother," I said.

I don't think I had called her "Mother" in years, and I had never said "shut up." "Shut up" was *her* comeback.

But she had stopped talking. She pulled in to the driveway, turned off the engine and got out of the driver's-side door without a word. The lights were off in the hangar and in my father's study, where Bernard and Milo slept, bright in Faith's room, where she was reading novels in Spanish.

I followed my mother through the front hall into the kitchen, where she turned off the light, down the corridor telling her good night as she went into her room and I went into Steven's. But she didn't respond.

In Stephen's room I waited until the sound of Julia's footsteps had disappeared and I could imagine her in bed, lying on her back so the cream didn't mess up the pillowcase, far on her side of the bed so her round body wouldn't intersect with my sleeping father. Her eyes would be wide open, staring at the ceiling.

I picked up the telephone and dialed Victor Duarte. It rang and rang, but there was no answer. No answering machine. I checked the clock. Almost midnight. I had been gone a long time. I called again, and still no answer. I lay down on the bed in my clothes, turned off the light and watched the second hand on the illuminated alarm clock move around the circle of passing time. At twelve-fifteen I called Victor again. No answer.

On the next try, I made myself wait, watching the minute hand move to 1:00 A.M., and then I called.

The phone rang and rang, maybe six or seven times, and then someone picked up, a silence, and Victor Duarte said, "Hello." I recognized his voice.

"This is Claire Frayn," I said. "I'm sorry to call so late."

"Oh, hello." His voice was flat.

"I called earlier, and you were out."

"I wasn't out. I was sleeping."

"I'm sorry to wake you."

"Never mind," he said wearily. "You've had a hard time."

"I wanted you to know I've made a decision about the photograph, remember? The man you showed me today—Benjamin Reed."

"Of course I remember."

"You said I should think about contacting him, yes?"

"If you wish. Only if you wish, is what I said."

"So I'm calling myself Sophia Lupe."

There was a long silence. Victor Duarte didn't seem to understand what I was saying at first, and then he did, and he laughed and laughed.

"Sophia Lupe, of course," he said.

THE LIFEGUARD CHAIR

Observations on Natural Selection from the Life Science Notebooks of Claire Frayn.

Industrial Melanism: *There are two types of English peppered moths (Biston betularia)—a light gray variety and a very dark one. In regions where the landscape was blackened when industrial pollution killed the lichens, the darker moths increased in relative number, and the lighter ones, without lichens to camouflage the color of their wings, were eaten by birds and nearly disappeared.*

"The case of Biston *reinforces the point that natural selection operates in the here and now, tending to adapt organisms to their local environment."**

My father—who fell in love with Darwin when he was a young student—told Steven and me about "survival of the fittest" as a bedtime story, as terrifying as any ghost story that Uncle Milo had to offer.

It was clear to me that of the two of us, Steven was the "fittest," that in an emergency I would crumple and die and he would sprout another arm,

---

*from my notes in reading *Biology* by Neil A. Campbell. —C.F.

grow more teeth, his breath would turn vile and poison the air around the enemy.

"You'll adapt," my father had said when I expressed concern about my own survival.

But I was not convinced.

C.F., age 14

White moth turning black

V.

THE EVOLUTION OF SOPHIA LUPE

I

Lisha had left a suitcase in Steven's closet, and the following morning I took it out. There were tops and a pair of tight jeans and a skimpy black skirt, a lacy magenta blouse, a blue-jean jacket and high-heeled black boots.

I had never dressed beyond necessity—working clothes, jeans, trousers, long-sleeved tees, occasionally a skirt. I didn't think about the way I looked or desire to change it. But standing in front of the full-length mirror on Steven's closet door, wearing Lisha's short black skirt and high-heeled boots and flimsy blouse, I felt a rush of interest in myself. I brushed my hair so it fell loose and a little wild around my face, put on makeup that Julia had gotten me, always hoping I'd make improvements. Black mascara and red-currant lipstick just beyond the lip line so my mouth looked fuller, blush high on my cheekbones.

To imagine myself a year ago, to re-create the physical memory of what it was like to live in this unstretched skin, is not possible for me now beyond the details of what happened. But I do remember that moment in Steven's mirror when I became a stranger to myself.

In the evenings when I was very young, my mother used to sit on her bed with me between her legs and read children's books in Spanish, and I was mesmerized by the mystery of a language I didn't know.

Imagining myself a year ago is like that.

Now I know the language, but I can't possibly resurrect a time before I could speak it.

Julia was in the kitchen making coffee, standing at the sink eating a piece of banana bread, Bernard limping down the hall from his bedroom.

"Interesting transformation," she said, assessing my new costume.

I poured a glass of orange juice and sat down.

"I hate the sound of Bernard's prosthesis clunking on the hardwood floor disturbing my peace," Julia said as he came in.

Bernard had become a repository for our family's anger. We had turned on him, all of us, even Faith.

"There's coffee on, and I put some banana bread in the oven to warm, Bern," Julia said.

He got breakfast and sat down next to me, cutting his banana bread in neat quarters.

"I want to mention something to you, Aunt Julia." And then a funny expression crossed his face, as if he were about to tell her but thought better of it.

"Too early for conversation, Bern. I'm heartsick this morning. You know what that word means? 'Heartsick'?"

"Yes, yes. I know 'heartsick.' "

He was quiet except for the gurgling in his throat, and I was about to get up because I couldn't stand the sound of it when he touched my arm. "Claire?"

"Yes, Bern."

"I notice you have bright lipstick on."

"I put it on this morning," I said. "Also mascara."

"It looks pretty, Claire," he said sweetly. "Very cheery."

"Thank you, Bernard." I was gentle with him, tried to be gentle, although there were times when I wanted to stuff his mouth with paper towels.

"There's something I need to say to you, Aunt Julia." Bernard was a short man, as his father had been, Eastern European in looks, with a wide brow and dark, curly hair, a large torso, short legs, short arms. He was nervous.

"I don't think you like me as much as you used to, and I want to do something about it."

Words he must have practiced that morning in the bathroom.

"You know, Bernard, I don't like anyone as much as I used to." Julia turned from the sink. "But of course I like you. I love you. And you drive me insane."

"How insane?" he asked in his earnest way.

"Very insane."

"Making that funny noise in your throat, Bernard," I said. I couldn't help myself. "You didn't used to do that."

"I'll stop, then," he said, getting up from the table, clearing his dishes. "I'll stop the noise today. I promise you that, Claire and Aunt Julia. Count on me."

He gathered his things for work and started out of the kitchen.

"Are you driving to school?" he asked me.

"I don't drive anymore," I said. "I thought you'd noticed that."

"I noticed that you don't drive, and then last night I asked Uncle Milo, and he said that's why he ordered a Rangely upright piano to be delivered on Friday afternoon this week." He checked the hall to see if Milo was opening the bedroom door to listen in on our conversation, as he liked to do. "To make everyone happy is why Milo got a piano, and when it comes, we'll be normal again and you'll be able to drive the car."

"Milo's raving mad," Julia said over the sound of water, cleaning out the sink. "A piano will ruin us."

Julia poured a cup of coffee from the fresh pot and sat down across from me, adding cream, swirling it into the coffee with her finger.

"Is he gone?"

"I don't hear him," I said.

"He makes me mentally ill."

She warmed her hands with the coffee cup breathing in the steam.

"So," she began, avoiding my eyes, hers focused on the wall, "I went into your bedroom for the first time yesterday."

I had been expecting this.

After I got rid of the animals and moved into Steven's bedroom, shutting the door to my own, I had only gone back once a day for the bird. The praying mantis had died, and I'd tossed her in the rose-bushes outside my door.

Julia had been too distracted to notice the changes I'd made, but I knew that one day she'd go into my bedroom and I would hear about it.

"Everything's gone except that stupid wingless bird."

"I know that."

"The plants are dead. Now, that's a waste of money."

I took a banana from the fruit bowl, wondering how much to say.

"I cleaned my room."

"What was to clean, Claire? That was your life, not just a room. You don't pack up your life in boxes."

"It's *my* life."

"And the stinking mice and the rat whose life you *promised* to save."

"The mice were field mice, and I put them in the field. I took the lab rat back to the lab."

"No you didn't," Julia said, looking at me directly, her eyes flashing. "You put it outside, probably in the garden. A domestic rat who had no idea how to fend for herself."

"Why do you ask if you already know?"

"I don't already know," she said. "I can just imagine you doing it."

She had gotten up from the table to dump her coffee in the sink.

"I can't take care of living things any longer," I said.

"In that case I'll make your room into a music room for Milo's miserable piano."

I put my dishes in the dishwasher, brushed the crumbs off the kitchen table and stuffed a bunch of grapes into the top of my backpack.

"Good idea?" she asked.

"It's your house," I said.

She was looking at me then, her cape over her shoulders, her purse and papers under her arm. "So is that what you're wearing to school today? A new persona. Why not?"

"These are Lisha's clothes," I said.

I could tell she was considering saying something mean and thinking better of it.

"I need a change," I said, stopping short of explaining myself.

"Your legs are too long for short skirts," she said. "But who am I to say?"

Milo had come into the kitchen, Bernard hurrying behind him.

"We have gang wars in Adams Morgan. I heard it on the radio," Milo announced.

"Gang wars," Bernard said, out of breath. "I heard it, too."

"Fighting on Columbia Road. They killed a bus driver last night. Be careful," Milo said to me.

"I don't go near Columbia Road," I said. "Don't worry about me."

"I don't worry about anyone any longer." My mother opened the back door. "Nothing to be gained."

I watched her car pull out of the driveway and then went back to Steven's bedroom, taking the letter I had written to Benjamin Reed from between the pages of *Civil Disobedience in Emerging Democracies*, where I'd slipped it before I went to sleep.

The book, turned to page 267, was on the table beside Steven's bed. At night when I couldn't sleep, I'd read those pages, my body filling the space on the bed he had occupied, believing that these pages were ones he had been reading the night before he died.

I zipped the letter into the pocket of my backpack and called Milo to say that I was on my way.

In the car Milo talked about his new piano and how he'd looked up the Mozart he wanted to play on the first evening the piano was in place between the windows in the living room—a sonata, number K.332, one he knew well and would play while Julia was cooking, the candles lit, the wine poured, the smell of dinner cooking, sometimes burning, he laughed.

We dropped Bernard off at the Tenleytown Metro and headed to Foggy Bottom.

"I have this plan, you see," Milo was saying. "Are you listening, Claire?"

"Yes, listening," I said, my face pressed to the glass, the windows half closed, the wind blowing my hair on top.

I was thinking of the conversation I would have with Victor Duarte as soon as I got to school.

We came into Washington Circle from Twenty-third Street, threaded our way through the rush-hour traffic headed downtown, and as we were exiting the other side of the circle beside the hospital, there was Victor walking alone just behind a group of young women, as if we had planned it this way.

"Stop here, Milo," I said, unbuckling my seat belt. "I just saw a friend."

"Here?"

"At the corner on Twenty-third. I'll walk to the library."

He pulled over, coming to a stop.

"I had so much more I wanted to tell you," he said. "Should I pick you up at six again?"

"I'll call you at home if I need a ride," I said, already thinking of plans with Victor. "I don't know how late I'll be."

Jumping out of the car, I waved good-bye and rushed ahead to catch up with Victor, my heart racing.

Milo's car was just out of view when Victor crossed my path, his hands in his pockets, walking at a clip.

"Victor," I called, threading through the crowd of students, and he turned around.

At first he looked at me as if we'd never met, his lips tight across his face, his eyes darker than I remembered, expressionless.

"Hi," I said quietly, and, feeling the need to introduce myself, added, "Remember? Claire Frayn."

"Of course I remember."

I fell in step.

"I just saw you through the window of my uncle's car and jumped out, hoping we could talk."

"I'd like to talk, but I'm in a hurry," he said. "Later, maybe."

"I have something to show you."

I was as tall as he was, but, walking beside him, I was taken by the size and strength of him, the hair on his arms, the weight of his jaw, his enormous hands.

"I'm headed to work," he said. "Later would be much better."

"We can't talk now at all?"

"Five minutes. No more or I'll be in trouble."

He tilted his head to the right, indicating a coffee shop, and I followed him in.

"I have this reputation for lateness," he said.

I slid into a booth and opened my book bag, taking out the letter I'd written.

"Aha." He opened the envelope. "So you wasted no time."

"The whole idea came to me last night when I was taking a walk in my neighborhood and got lost. I was thinking Sophia Lupe should be a good Catholic girl, proper and faithful but longing for something more."

"A provocative novitiate, yes?"

"I don't know the word 'novitiate.' "

"A student nun in training for her marriage to Jesus. You understand 'provocative'?"

"Yes. Sophia is provocative."

"That's all you need to know."

He read the letter quickly and put it back in the envelope. "You're an actress," he said, narrowing his eyes. "I could tell when I met you that you were a closet actress."

"Oh, no I'm not. I'm a terrible actress," I said.

A literalist is how I had always thought of myself. Someone who looked at the visible world as the final truth. But what did I know? My familiar body, long legs, short torso, small shoulders, no flesh. My turn of mind for natural history was in the process of changing. No telling what new character might be revealed. Perhaps Victor Duarte could see things in me beyond what I knew of myself.

"You'll need to set up a box at the post office in Foggy Bottom, since you don't want letters from Benjamin Reed coming to your home. Send the letter in care of the music department at the University of Michigan in Ann Arbor and cross your fingers."

"Do you like what I wrote?"

He smiled, getting up to leave. "If I were Benjamin Reed, I'd be on the next plane."

I leaned back against the leather cushion of the booth, laying my hand lightly on top of his, surprised at my own boldness.

"You've given me a mission," I said quietly.

"*Our* mission," he said, taking his hand away. "I loved Steven Frayn like a brother."

I believed him. When I consider now why I would have trusted a stranger, when the complications and clues and foolish chances I took without a second thought roll through my mind like the credits at the end of a movie, what I did is still possible to understand.

I *needed* to believe him. I had lost my way.

Victor got up from the booth and put down a dollar tip on the table.

"I'm off now," he said. "We'll be in touch. But carefully, you understand."

"I don't exactly understand," I said.

"The FBI is looking for your brother's murderer. That's right isn't it?"

"They call with questions and come over to speak to my parents. Maybe once a week. But I'd never tell them about Benjamin, if that's what you mean."

"It'd be normal for you to tell them that we've met, that I've suggested Benjamin Reed might *know* who killed Steven. They look for leads."

"So you want us to do this mission by ourselves?" I asked. "Is that what you're saying?"

"That's what I mean," he said.

At the Foggy Bottom branch of the post office, where I went after I left the coffeehouse and before chemistry, arriving late to lab, I paid three months in advance for Box 1330, addressed the envelope to *"Benjamin Reed, Music Department, University of Michigan, Ann Arbor"*—writing in a loopy, romantic hand instead of my usual small, crabbed cursive—wrote *"S. Lupe, Box 1330,"* et cetera, got stamps and stuck the letter in the slot marked OTHER DESTINATIONS.

As I walked though the front door of the post office onto the street, the wind lifted my skirt and I felt a rush of exhilaration. For a moment on this crystal blue morning in May, I had reclaimed my future from Steven's death.

2

When I arrived home, the Rangely upright had been delivered and Milo was playing Mozart. The living room was dark except for the light beside the piano and smelled of broccoli cooking.

I dropped my backpack in the hall and leaned into the living room to find Bernard sitting on the couch with his hands folded as if he were at a public concert and must comport himself.

"The FBI is here." He put his finger to his lips.

"Why are they here at dinner?"

"It's important. They're in the kitchen with your parents."

The agents were standing side by side, their backs against the sink.

"Agents Brownstein and Burns," the older of the two said, indicating the smaller birdlike man as Burns.

I nodded, sliding into the empty chair next to Lisha.

"I was saying to your parents that we're sorry to interrupt your dinner hour. We've come up with some news, not much, but as a result we need more information from you."

My father had pushed his chair away from the table, tipped it back and seemed to be asleep.

"There was a group," Julia said to me under her breath. "Remember when I said there was a group and asked you to find out from Steven whether he had belonged to any group we didn't know about?"

"I remember."

"I was right. There was one."

"The group is called DTT, which stands for Demand Tolerance Today. Do any of you know of it?" Agent Burns asked.

My heart was beating in my throat. I knew about DTT from Victor and glanced at Lisha to see if she, too, had heard of the group, but she showed no sign.

"As far as we can determine, it's a national human-rights organization of young left-wing Democrats who take issue with the Justice Department's position on immigration, among other things." Agent Brownstein turned to me. "Still haven't heard of it?"

I shook my head.

"They have a Web site, and some of Steven's essays appear there. Check DTT.com."

My mother wrote "DTT.com" under "dairy" on her grocery list.

"The people we spoke to at the Civil Rights Division had heard of it, but they showed no particular interest, so we think it's just one of a million political fraternities. Nothing of significance," Agent Burns said.

My father pulled his chair back up to the table.

"The reason we're here tonight without any notice is a follow-up of the autopsy report that got to us today."

"I don't know that I can listen," my father said, but he didn't get up.

"It'll be quick," Agent Burns, the gentler of the two, said, as if quick would make a difference.

Julia sat on the edge of her chair with the back of the grocery list on the table, taking notes.

The medical examiner's report indicated that the bullet entered

Steven's head at an angle, which suggested it had been shot from quite close proximity and below the steps where Steven would have been standing.

Agent Brownstein drew a diagram, with an arrow representing the bullet entering Steven's head.

My father stood up, his hands in his pockets, and paced.

"We've determined that the bullet came from a small storage room with a window in the basement of Phillips Hall. The window has a clear view of the entrance to the library."

"What does that mean?" my father wanted to know.

"It means that we have evidence to continue exploring the possibility that Steven was an *intentional* target."

"What do you need from us?" My father was visibly shaken, anxious for the FBI men to leave.

"More names. As many as you can think of who might have known your son," Agent Brownstein said.

"I told you everyone I could remember," Julia said.

"What about neighbors?" Agent Burns asked. "You live in a transient neighborhood, so you've had a lot of neighbors in and out."

"I'll try to remember more," Julia said.

"We found the teacher you mentioned, but he didn't remember Steven or much else. Early-onset dementia." Agent Burns had walked across the kitchen toward the door, and we all stood to say good-bye.

"The profile of Steven we've assembled so far is one of an outspoken, sometimes brash young man willing to have some enemies along the way." Agent Brownstein's voice was matter-of-fact. "We're in search of enemies."

"Or a problem," Agent Burns said. "A window into some undercover life he might have had, and we can't seem to find one."

"He didn't reveal himself to everyone." I was upset by all the questioning, which intrinsically had a suggestion of blame. "He was close to his family. To us. To each of us."

"That's very clear," they said, and after polite exchanges with Lisha and my parents, they left.

"Is it true that people didn't know Steven?" Julia asked my father after the FBI agents had left.

"*We* didn't know him well enough, or we would have known he was in some kind of trouble."

Lisha leaned forward at the table, speaking for the first time since I'd come into the kitchen.

"He kept everything to himself," she said. "Even with all his talking—and he loved to talk—it was never personal."

"I knew Steven," I said, conscious of the thinness of my voice. "I knew him completely."

But I had already come to realize that wasn't true.

Bernard stopped me as I headed to my room. "Do they have a suspect?"

"They don't," I said, stiffening as he followed me into Steven's room and sat down beside me on the edge of the bed.

"But it's already been six weeks," he said.

"They just got the autopsy report and think it's possible that Steven was an intentional target."

"You mean someone wanted to kill him?"

"That's what I mean."

I left the bed and sat down at Steven's desk, busying myself with papers from school, hoping Bernard wouldn't stay long.

"Do you think it's strange that Steven and I both had accidents, two of us in one American family, and no one ever talks about it? Not even my mother."

"*Yours* was an accident, Bernard," I said patiently, trying to be careful with him because he loved me and I didn't want to hurt him. "Someone who didn't know Bernard Wendt, didn't know that he'd be coming into the 7-Eleven at five-fifteen that afternoon, minutes after the culprit had put a small explosive behind the cereal boxes. You just happened to be picking up Cheerios when the bomb went off, blasting the 7-Eleven so a girder fell on your leg. It was an accident."

"I know what happened because I was there."

"Steven was different. He was killed by someone who wanted to kill him, and that's not an accident."

"I just think it's strange and upsetting."

"It *is* strange and upsetting."

"Sometimes I get very confused, Claire." He got up from the bed. "That's why I'm glad you're my cousin," he said, smiling at me sweetly, as he did even when I was having the most terrible thoughts about him. I should have reached out and hugged him then, which was what he wanted from me, but I turned away and opened my chemistry book, listening for him to leave.

After Bernard was gone, I called the number Victor had given me, which a recording said was out of service. I tried it again and received the same report. When I checked, the operator said the number had been disconnected. I looked up Duarte in the phone book. There was one Victor in northeast Washington—three months dead, according to the woman who answered the phone. I called a V. Duarte without an address but didn't leave a message when the voice on the answering machine was foreign. There were two other Duartes, Martin on First Street and Estella on Livingston. I was copying their numbers in a notebook when Lisha walked in.

"Thank God the FBI left," I said. "I hated what they said about Steven."

"That he didn't have close friends? He didn't. Just girlfriends and admirers."

She reached into the closet, took out the suitcase she had left there and opened it.

"I'm wearing your clothes," I said. "I hope you don't mind."

"You can have all of them if you'd like," she said, an edge of irritation in her voice.

She wrapped her arms around her chest.

"I wish you weren't so pleasant, Claire. You're always so pleasant," she said. "Be difficult. Everyone else is difficult."

I sat down on the edge of Steven's bed, taking off my glasses so Lisha was a satisfying blur.

"What you should say to me is, 'I like these clothes, Lisha, and I'm going to be wearing them from now on.'" Her pretty face was scrunched into a cartoon. "It drove Steven crazy that you are such a—" She stopped, dumped the clothes from the suitcase on the bed and closed it.

"Such a what?"

"Such a little girl."

The telephone rang before I had a chance to respond.

That little girl is dead, is what I could have said, except Julia came into the room to say that the call was for me.

3

Victor's voice had the hollow, tinny sound of an older woman's, so I hesitated when he asked me to meet him at Union Station in forty-five minutes, in front of the fountain at the main entrance.

"I'm at a pay phone in the Metro," he said. "My phone's out."

"I know," I said. "I called."

"Disconnected. I've moved. I'll tell you about it when I see you."

My mother was putting dinner on the table when I hung up.

"The broccoli's mush." She dumped it in a bowl. "I cooked it too long."

I took a stalk and dipped it in salt.

"It tastes fine."

"Salty." She turned to look at me. "I heard you say 'Victor.'"

"He's a friend from school," I lied, checking the hook next to the back door where we kept the car keys. "He's helping me get through finals, since I missed so much time."

"I've never heard of him."

"You wouldn't. There's nothing to say, except he's a good student and helps me out."

She raised her eyebrows, dissatisfied with my explanation. "Faith's coming home late, so we're eating without her."

"Without me, too," I said quickly.

She looked up from the cutting board where she was slicing chicken. "You haven't eaten."

"I'm going to GW to study."

"With this person? This Victor?"

I picked up my book bag, slipped the keys to Steven's Toyota into the pocket of my skirt and went out the back door.

"I'll be back by midnight," I called.

"Midnight," Julia repeated. "How are you getting downtown?"

"Driving."

"You don't drive," she said, sinking into a chair, her head in her hand.

"I drive," I said.

My father met up with me on his way in from the hangar.

"So I see Milo got his piano in spite of my request," he said.

"It's a small piano. You'll learn to like it," I said, hooking my arm through his. "Do you mind if I take Steven's car to study at GW?"

"You'll drive alone?"

"You don't mind, do you?"

"I don't mind, of course." He reached out and touched my hair. "But you haven't driven at all since April. Does this mean you're feeling stronger?"

"Stronger? Yes, I suppose I'm feeling stronger."

"I'm glad. I'm very glad. We must . . ."

He didn't go on, but I could feel him watching me as I crossed the lawn.

It was almost dark, late spring, the days lengthening, and I climbed into the front seat of the car, turned the key in the ignition, switched on the lights and backed out.

Mr. Denver, whose interest in our family's tragedy had not diminished, was on his front lawn checking his garden. He waved at me, and I opened the window.

"Any luck?" he called.

"Luck?"

"Any good luck finding the criminal?" He gave me a complicit smile, and I wanted to kill him.

It occurred to me that I could turn left, go over the curb and run Mr. Denver down in his own front yard. I had a picture in my mind of the event.

Mr. Denver would be lying on his back, dead on impact with Steven's Toyota. I would back out, drive in the direction of Washington, and someplace around Massachusetts Avenue and Sheridan Circle the police would stop me to ask if I had information that might lead to the hit-and-run driver who killed Mr. Denver.

I would say, "It was me." Or "It was I." I've always had trouble with grammar. And the policeman would thank me and wave me on my way.

I pulled out of the driveway and headed in the direction of River

Road, my eyes fixed straight ahead, then turned onto River Road, right on Wisconsin, left at the arrow onto Massachusetts. I was almost downtown before I realized that I had actually been driving a car for the first time since Steven died.

Killing Mr. Denver had occupied that much of my time.

Victor was pacing by the fountain when I arrived. He got into the passenger seat, closed the door, folded his arms tight across his chest.

"Where're we going?"

"To the movies," he said.

"What movie?" I asked.

"Any movie," he said. "I don't care."

He was agitated, his feet tapping, his head turning this way and that, nervous about going out with me, but I wasn't necessarily surprised or even on guard. I liked that he seemed to be a complicated man. It made me feel interesting.

I drove up the ramp to the open deck, with a view of Washington spread out around us like a toy city. The parking lot was dimly lit, the deck empty of people, silent so far above the city.

Walking beside Victor, I swung my arms back and forth, hoping my hand would intersect with his. I wasn't sure what to expect of the evening, but I expected something, was ready for whatever happened, physically stronger, my flesh in the process of hardening.

As we got on the escalator, our hands did meet palm to palm, and he slid his into the pockets of his trousers and kept them there.

There were six films playing at the Union Station multiplex and we stood for awhile, early for the films, looking at the selection.

"What do you think?" I asked.

"I want some french fries," he said, and so we sat on high stools in the food court on the lower level of Union Station next to the cinemas, eating french fries and drinking beer.

He asked what had been going on, and I told him about the FBI and the findings from the autopsy.

"So do they think it was one gunman or more?" he asked, lighting up with interest.

"One shot, but they didn't say. Only that the gun was fired from a small room with a window looking up at the library steps."

"That's odd," Victor said, but he was distracted, his eyes traveling the mall.

"Odd?"

"That's what I said."

"Odd that they think his death was intentional?"

"I'm sure it was intentional. I'm just surprised that whoever did it was copying Lee Harvey Oswald. Remember? Risky, you know. Right next to the university library. All those students. So close he could have been caught."

"You think it *was* Benjamin Reed."

"I didn't say that. I don't know. I only know as much as I told you."

"But we'll find out, yes?"

"I think we will."

We went into the nine o'clock showing of a movie called *Rose*.

"Do you know what it's about?" I asked.

"Nope," he replied. "I like anything Maya Flora is in."

The movie was about a convent in Brazil, and I don't remember it at all, so perhaps I fell asleep, but when the credits started to roll, Victor got up to leave without even looking at me, as if he were sleepwalking, lost in thought, disappearing into the departing crowd.

I got stuck behind a group of people who moved slowly up the aisle, and by the time I came into the food court outside the theater, he was already on the escalator.

"Hey," I said, catching up.

"I thought you were right behind me," he said. He checked his watch.

"It's not so late," I said.

I had thought we would go to a bar after the movie, or get ice cream and coffee, maybe stop by his new place.

"I've got to head home," he said.

"Where is that?"

"I've got a place near the station."

"We can have a drink in one of the bars upstairs in the station."

"I've got work to do for DTT," he said when we'd reached the top of the escalator and the exit to North Capitol Street.

"Maybe you could walk me to my car." I wondered if something had gone wrong, something I had done. "The roof deck is creepy in the dark."

I was beginning to feel as if we'd just met and there was nothing between us. That I'd mistaken his intentions and he hadn't asked me to meet him at the movie theater with any intentions beyond the movie, although surely there'd been expectation in his voice.

Or was it *me* with expectations? I wondered. And this desire for Victor Duarte was *my* longing, not Victor's, and only tangled in Steven's death. How did a woman know the origin of particular attraction, or did it matter? I understood so little of the world.

"You're right," he said. "It's risky at night on the roof deck. Not enough light."

He followed me up the next escalator and the next until we had reached the roof parking deck.

Inside the car he fiddled with the dial until he found a music station and then turned it off.

"I'm a little nervous," he said. "I'm like that sometimes, and I've got a lot going on, stuff with my job. Since I started working with DTT, I have a double life. You understand?"

"I don't."

"By day I'm an engineer and spend my lunch hour in the library reading law, and by night I'm like a detective."

It was cold and dark in the garage, and I drew my shoulders in, shivering.

"Steven had enemies," he was saying. "He could upset people. You know that. It's why we're pursuing Benjamin Reed."

"I do know he had enemies."

I waited until he was settled in the passenger seat.

"Will you give me your new telephone number before I let you off?" I asked.

"I'm using a cell phone instead of a landline in my new place," he said.

"But I can call you on that number?"

"I'll call *you* in a few days to check what you've heard from Benjamin."

"A few days?"

"I'm very busy, Claire."

"I thought we were partners."

I felt as if something inevitable that had been in the process of happening between us was dissolving.

"We are partners, but I work in the field like a plumber. I'm never at the office."

We were headed down the parking ramp.

"You're still interested in our mission together, aren't you?" I was tentative.

"It means the world to me," he said and to my surprise, his voice was suddenly full of emotion.

I believed him and was physically relieved. Just a slip of misunderstanding between us, I thought. Nothing to worry over.

He opened the door and got out at the corner of North Capitol, waving his hand for me to wait, leaning into the open passenger window.

"I was thinking something tonight while we were watching the movie."

His face was close enough to mine for me to feel his breath.

"I was wondering, what have you done with Steven's clothes?"

"Nothing. They're still in his closet," I said. "We've done nothing yet."

"It's too soon," he said. "I know it's too soon, but when you're ready, I'd like to have something of his."

"Like clothes? Or something else?"

"Like clothes," he said. "Something tangible."

It was a sweet request, and the intimacy of it made up for his distance that evening.

"Of course," I replied, moved to think of him wearing Steven's clothes, wanting to wear them. "You and Steven must have been very good friends."

"We were, and you can call me V," he said. "It's what your brother called me."

And then he raised his hand in a gesture like benediction, and I watched him walk down Massachusetts Avenue, turn right and disappear into the darkness.

4

When I got home after midnight, the Web site for DTT was up on Steven's computer.

"Check this out. J," my mother had written on a yellow sticky she'd stuck to the screen.

I scrolled down the index.

There was a category for membership in the column on the left of the Web page. I opened it and typed in *Steven Frayn.* His name wasn't listed among the members.

This didn't surprise me. Steven had never joined groups, even in high school when everyone we knew belonged to something. It wasn't in our "family character," according to my father, who liked to think such a thing as collective family character existed.

What did surprise me was that Victor Duarte wasn't included among the list of members.

Under "General Information," I found my brother.

There were four of his articles from the *Washington Post* and the *Law Review* at George Washington University, all pieces related to the recent treatment of immigrants, including the last piece on the Freedom Act that had appeared in the *Post* the day he died. His obituary in the *Post* was there, the notice in the news section of the *New York Times* and a couple of investigative stories that had appeared in various newspapers. There were letters posted by people all over the country—mostly members of DTT, but others as well, especially students.

I was reading the letters and didn't hear the knock at my door or my mother walk in without waiting for me to answer. She was dressed for the day, although it was just after three in the morning.

"You got home late," she said.

"Twelve forty-nine. I checked the clock."

She leaned over my chair, reading what was on the screen. "Never mind. Stay out all night. It's your life."

I pulled my chair away from the desk so she could have a clear view. "Where are *you* going?" I asked.

"To work."

"Now? It's the middle of the night."

"Soon enough," she said.

"Did you go to bed at all tonight?"

"I waited for you, and then I had some things to do." She straightened and walked across the room, closing the door to Steven's closet, where I'd been going through his clothes. "Steven's not on the membership list. Did you notice?"

"I noticed."

"I read those letters, too," she said, indicating the entries I'd been reading. "He was a hero."

"I guess he was."

"I doubt they're going to find out who killed him. That's my opinion. They'll look around for a while and find nothing."

"Why do you think that?"

"After the FBI left, I told your father there's not a chance."

"And what did he say?" I asked.

"He said to wait. 'Wait' is your father's favorite word." She picked up a photograph of Lisha on Steven's bureau and turned it facedown. "We're going to give the FBI this long list of people Steven has known, none of them significant as suspects, and a couple of years from now they'll conclude that it was an accident or the bullet was intended for someone else. I can't think about it."

"They said it wasn't an accident."

"Of course it wasn't, but no one's going to find that out, I promise. No one will find the killer."

I wanted to tell her about Benjamin Reed. I wanted to say that with Victor's help I was in the process of discovering who had killed Steven, so she'd know there was a chance for retribution.

Something in the lateness of the night, the two of us together, wakeful conspirators, while everyone in the house was sleeping, encouraged me. A matter of pride to say I knew.

But I said nothing.

"Does it matter if they find him?" Julia sat down on the edge of Steven's bed. "Does it matter to you?"

"It matters if we find out it wasn't an accident. That matters very much." My face was suddenly hot with rising anger.

"Your father favors enemies, too." She reached into the pocket of her skirt and pulled out a piece of sketching paper. "I'm designing a glass for Steven."

She handed me the design, and under the light on Steven's desk it looked like a treble clef in cerulean blue. An *S* with an upside-down *F* within the half circles.

"On clear glass," Julia said. "Can you tell what it says?"

"S.F.," I said.

"Should I include a note with the glasses when people buy them? Something like '*In memory of Steven Frayn*'?"

"I'd let them think it's a treble clef."

She put the sketch back in her pocket and headed toward the door on her way out of the room.

And then she hesitated.

"Something's going on with you, isn't it, Claire?" Her arms were folded across her chest, pulling her broad shoulders close together, a smaller woman than I always thought of her, and I wished that I could be comfortable with some gesture of affection, but I could not.

There was too much sadness between us.

"Something's going on with all of us, Mama," I said.

At the computer I searched DTT for Victor Duarte again.

I tried V. Duarte. Nothing.

Perhaps I had misunderstood. Victor may have only mentioned DTT by way of explanation. I couldn't remember if he said he was a member or not.

I looked up Charles Reed, and there were many entries, most recently an editorial in the *New York Times* on his position restricting immigration and stiffening requirements for a green card. Nothing on Benjamin except the photograph Victor had shown me at his father's swearing-in ceremony, which I looked up in the archives of the *Washington Post*'s Web site.

I was still at the computer when my mother left the house. She backed out of the driveway and turned left at the Denvers', the lights in her car shining through the window of Steven's room.

The bed was made in her room when I went in, and I doubted that it had been slept in at all that night. On my father's pillow that he no longer used—he slept instead on a futon in the hangar—there was a note.

> *Dear David.*
>> *I have moved to the glass factory.*
>>> *Te amo. Julia*

THE LIFEGUARD CHAIR

After dinner Stephen usually agrees to play a board game called FROGS that my father made as a present for me one Christmas. But lately, at Stephen's insistence, we've been having serious conversations about moral consequences instead. Our conversations, which he calls arguments, usually begin with "What if."

"So, Claire," he'll say just as I'm beginning my Algebra homework or planning to call Eva, "what if you are in Cambodia during the time of the Khmer Rouge. You have the chance to save the Roo family, but the price of it—the saving of four children, two parents and a grandfather—will be the sacrifice of your own life."

"I'd save my own life," I reply.

"Bad choice," he says.

"I don't know the Khmer Rouge, so why would I want to save the Roos from them?"

He tries again.

"Let's say your best friend has robbed the 7-Eleven of two cartons of vitamin-D milk and a jumbo package of peanut M&M's Do you turn her in to the police?"

"What difference does it make to you?" I asked. "My best friend is Eva, and she'd split the M&M's with me."

I drive him crazy in these conversations.

"Sometimes I wonder if you have any moral consciousness," he says.

"I don't want one," I say.

But Steven is persistent.

"We'll start again," he says. "What if you're living in a village in Germany during the Second World War, and you know that the Jews are dying in the furnaces near your town. You can even see the smoke. What do you do?"

"What did the people in the village do?" I ask.

"Why do you need to know about other people? This question is for you."

"I'd do nothing. I'm not a policeman."

"Are you telling me you'd just let the Germans burn up the Jews while you sit in your kitchen happily eating your chocolate pudding and drinking Orange Crush and playing with your yellow haired friends without a care in the world?"

"I'm telling you I don't like this game," I say, my eyes full of tears.

"It's not a game," he says.

"That's why I don't like it," I say. "I like the old games we used to play, like FROGS."

C.F., age 14, ninth grade

My own private frog game

VI.

ADAPTATION

I

The letter from Benjamin Reed came a week after I had finished my makeup exams and was working a few hours a day with summer-school students in the biology lab. It came in a brown business envelope, handwritten, *"Sophia Lupe"* in a large, scrawling script, the letters leaning backward, so he must be left-handed, I concluded.

I had not heard from Victor at all, except once late at night when he gave me the number for his new cell phone, asking me not to call until Benjamin had been in touch. He had been very busy with his job, he said, and hung up. I left a message on his voice mail asking him to call back, it was important. Which he didn't do.

On the Friday afternoon that Benjamin's letter arrived, I called again before I'd even left the post office and got his voice mail.

"The letter is here," I said, walking outside, leaning against the brick wall of the post-office building.

When he didn't call back immediately, I dialed his number again. "Should I open Benjamin's letter now or wait for you to call?"

In the lab I left the phone off.

"Open it," his message said. "And get back to me."

After class I sat on a cement bench in a small garden outside the life-sciences building and opened the letter.

It was warm and clear, the sun just overhead, but I was shivering in spite of the heat.

Dear Sophia Lupe,

What a mysterious surprise you should find me. And then all of these coincidences between us.

I'm so sorry about your brother's death. I know it has been an unbearable loss.

I'm living in Ann Arbor studying musical composition at the university and as it happens living a lonely life, although no one would ever guess that of me, since I am by training loquacious—my father in politics, my mother Latin and a musician of such temperament that I can still remember her kissing me good night although she's been dead since I was six.

I'm glad, however, to be in Michigan, especially to be out of Washington, an unpredictable city short on friendship.

That's a little about me. Maybe there's only a little to know beyond what follows.

PRELUDE I:

Your letter inspired this composition. It can be played on an upright piano, even an inexpensive one.

    Yours, Benjamin

I dialed Victor.

"It's music," I said.

"What do you mean, music?"

"Benjamin only wrote a few actual words, and they say nothing."

I read him the text.

"The rest is music," I said.

"Damn." I could hear excitement in his voice. "What do you
know about music?"

"Nothing. What about you?"

He laughed. "I certainly can't read music," he said.

"I do have an uncle who's a concert pianist, the one who picked
me up the first time we met."

"Then you must have access to a piano?"

"A new one. Milo just got it."

"Go home and have your uncle play Benjamin's letter for you."

There was street noise in the background, and I had to strain to
hear him.

"Then I'll call you?" I asked.

"Call me tomorrow, and we'll meet after I finish work."

"I'll bring the letter."

"And bring your answer to it."

I stuffed Benjamin's letter back in the envelope. "How do you answer a song?" I asked.

A woman had sat down next to me on the bench, and I got up, walking toward the sidewalk.

"You told him you were a student of musical composition, so he'll expect you to be able to write a song."

"I did say that, but how can I do it?"

"Your uncle will make up songs on his new piano."

I walked along a sidewalk crowded with students, weaving through them, pressing the phone against my ear, thinking how happy it would make Uncle Milo to have the job of writing a song for me.

I was in a charade, a kind of high-stakes fifty-two pickup in which the cards, tossed in the air, fluttered to the ground, and I didn't bother to pick them up or try to set them in order, too separated from myself to be concerned with consequences.

2

Milo was playing the piano when I got home, and I imagined he had been playing all day. The house was empty—Faith and Bernard at work, my mother relocated to the glass factory, my father in the hangar.

It was early afternoon, not even three, and since my final exams had gone better than I'd expected, I had a meeting with my adviser for next semester's courses. But after the letter came from Benjamin, I didn't have the patience to stay at school.

I slid down on the piano bench beside Milo.

"Now, listen. I'm playing my own song," he said, stopping mid-tune. "I wrote it today, and you'll be surprised at how good it is for a stale musician."

"Play it," I said, hardly able to contain myself.

"Don't complain if it isn't perfect."

"I won't *know* if it isn't perfect."

"Oh, yes you will," he said, throwing his head back, stretching his hands with the long, long fingers across the keys, assuming the seriousness of a public concert.

"It's quite a sad song, isn't it?" I asked when he had finished playing.

"I meant it to be hopeful." He spread his arms in a gesture of despair. "Didn't you hear the hopeful?"

"Perhaps I didn't listen well enough."

"I'll play it again. Listen carefully." He played, looking over at me when the tempo picked up, his fingers running up the scale. "See?" he said. "Hopeful."

"I must have been preoccupied."

I wanted to get on with my letter and was wondering how to make this experiment with Milo work. I wasn't ordinarily a good liar.

"This time I heard the hopeful," I said.

I unfolded the letter, flattening the paper, and handed it to Milo. I had already cut the musical score out of the body of Benjamin's letter so Milo wouldn't see the name Sophia Lupe and inquire about her.

"I have a friend who wrote a song for me," I began.

"A boyfriend."

"Not yet," I said.

"You want me to play this?" He put it up on the piano.

"I was thinking you could play and we could listen to it together and then you could compose a response for me to send back to him."

"So romantic," he said, laughing. "I had no idea that you, the scientist, with all your treasured carcasses, could be a genuine romantic."

He leaned over the piano keys, squinting to see the notes on Benjamin's composition.

"Aha! Like me. He must be a confirmed romantic to the core, or he wouldn't write such a song."

He cocked his head to the side, as if he were favoring one ear for listening, his thick, fuzzy eyebrows raised.

When he had finished playing, he rested his hands in his lap, and then he played the melody again.

"What do you think?" I asked.

"It's lyrical and very sweet," he said. "If you plan to make him your boyfriend, he's a good candidate based on this composition."

"He's a student of music."

"The song has the sound of 'Careless Love,' don't you think? Something in the syncopation."

"I can't remember 'Careless Love.' "

" 'Love, oh love, oh careless love.' La, la, la, la, la, la, la," he sang.

"I think his is different," I said, listening carefully, something I hadn't done with music before. "More lalala. LA, LA, LAAAA."

"You're perfect, Claire, an instinctive musician. LA, LA, LAAAA. I think he must have written the song for you alone." He zipped his fingers up the scale. "You alone, you alone, are the dream I have known. Beautiful you, you, you." He stood and bowed. "Thank you everyone. Thank you," he said, sitting back down beside me. "It's funny and playful, and he calls it Prelude I." He slapped his hands together. "Next there'll be Prelude II."

"If I write him back in music, yes?" I said with feigned innocence. "Do you think you could compose a response?"

"A response, aha."

"A song like his to me, in the same spirit. I want him to believe I'm a musician, too."

"And why does he need to believe you are a musician, Claire?"

"Because I told him I was."

"You wicked child. Lying at the beginning of a love affair." Milo shook his head. "My mistake. Always that was my mistake. Lie at the beginning, and then you're trapped."

"I wanted him to think we had something important in common."

"Of course, but you could have pretended something other than music. Music is hard to make up," he said, moving his fingers lightly up the scale. "And now you want me to write him a song as if you had written it."

"That is what I want," I said.

"You're lucky I'm your uncle." He took my hand and kissed the fingers. "So I'll make up a song, immediately, now, before dinner." He rubbed his own hands together. "Something flirty?"

I nodded.

"Subtle. Just a rustle of the skirt, a *click-click-click* of high heels on the pavement. Flirty, yes?"

And he began to play, starting, stopping, his head bobbing back and forth until I could hear a melody surfacing in the notes, a kind of dance song.

"Too melancholy," he said, running his fingers through his hair. "It needs to be lighter. Whimsical is what we're after. Kiss, kiss, kiss. Nothing more than a kiss brushing the lips, yes?"

And he'd change a few notes, play the song again and again.

"Almost perfect," he said just as Faith arrived from work. "What do you think?"

"I think it's wonderful," I said. "Is it wonderful?"

"It's brilliant," he said. "I'm a genius."

After dinner Milo wrote out the song on staff paper and gave it to me.

"This is our secret," I said. "You won't tell anyone, will you?"

"To the future," he said with a flourish. "And I'll tell no one."

"Are you teaching Claire piano?" Bernard asked, coming into the living room after dinner.

"Claire wants to be a composer," Milo said. "I'm teaching her about composition."

"I thought you wanted to be a biologist, Claire."

"I may be changing my mind."

"I liked it when you were a biologist and your room was full of dead things. I used to go in to look at them, especially the kitten with the white neck."

"I know you liked the kitten, Bernard."

"And now that's over, and you're going to be a composer."

"I'm hoping to be a composer," I said, heading to my room.

In the bedroom I called Victor.

"I'm coming over to your house," I said. "I have the letter."

There was a long pause.

"When are you coming?" he asked.

"Now," I said. "My uncle has written the song for Benjamin, and also I have something I want to give you."

He gave me directions to his new apartment, but he was vague about our arrangements, as if he didn't know whether he would be there when I arrived. I could hardly hear him speak.

"You'll be at home when I get there?"

"I'm not sure. I'm very busy, and we *had* planned to meet tomorrow."

"But I want you to see the letter."

"Then I suppose you can come," he said. "But carefully."

"Carefully?"

"I don't live in the best part of town."

After I hung up, I pulled out the second drawer of Steven's bureau, where he kept his shirts. His favorite T-shirts were stacked on one shelf. On the top of the stack was his debate-team tee, dark green, the cotton thin with washings.

FRAYN was written on the back of the shirt and, underneath, CAPTAIN—WALT WHITMAN HIGH SCHOOL DEBATE TEAM.

3

Capitol Hill was barricaded around the Capitol and the Supreme Court, cement barriers between the buildings and the street where lawn had been. Police gathered in groups, stopping cars as they passed, checking the backseats, the trunks, chatting casually.

Victor had moved northeast of the Capitol, on Thirteenth Street between Tennessee and North Carolina, beyond the barriers— 922 Thirteenth Street NE, the lower level of a town house, he had told me.

He told me to stop in front of 922, ring the basement apartment, marked B next to the bell, and if he didn't answer right away to call him on his cell phone.

I found Thirteenth Street, but I couldn't seem to find 922, so I double-parked the car, got out and walked, leaving the engine running across from 916, a row house with lights on the second floor. Number 918 had an outside light, so I was able to see the numbers beside the front door, but 920 was dark, and when I walked up the front steps, the door was boarded shut. There was no 922. The next house, 924, was lit, the television playing so loud I could hear it clearly on the street.

Otherwise the street was empty and silent, not even the sound of cars passing through. I could hear my flip-flops slapping the asphalt.

I should have been afraid, but I was not.

I walked back to 916, where the second-floor light had been on, hoping the occupants knew which one was Victor's house, but when I knocked, the light upstairs went out.

Maybe I had misheard the address, although certainly he had said

Thirteenth Street. The number 922 stuck in my head, but it could have been 942—and just as I was getting into the driver's seat to call Victor, someone from across the street called out, "GIRL!"

The night was damp and thick, not raining yet, and the humidity dulled the tunnel of light from the streetlamps.

I should have had the sense to drive away, but I had no fear then, not of the streets or this voice on the street or of Victor—I was courting danger, hoping for trouble, testing the limits of fate. After Steven's death nothing more could harm me.

"Yes?" I replied to the ghost in the dark who had called me "girl."

"You're looking in the wrong direction."

The voice was rolling, southern, male.

I turned the other way, and then I saw him. A man in shadows walking toward me. Young, in sloppy jeans and a jacket, a swagger to his step.

"What're you doing out here in the middle of the night?"

"I'm meeting a friend."

He stepped just short of the light from the streetlamp, so I couldn't see his face.

"A friend." It wasn't a question. "And what would be your friend's name?"

"Victor Duarte. He knows I'm coming. He's looking out the window for me and will be here any minute."

"Victor Duarte doesn't live on this block of Thirteenth Street. I know everyone on this block, and I've never heard of him."

"Maybe I got the address wrong." I was suddenly uneasy, and I shut the car door, locked it, put the car in drive.

My cell phone was ringing.

"Where are you?" Victor asked.

I was driving then to the end of the block, past the stranger who had continued down the middle of the road, probably high on something, turning right in the direction of the Capitol.

"There *is* no 922."

"There is," he said. "You must have missed it, so come around the block again and I'll meet you in the street."

I followed his directions, and as soon as I rounded the corner, I saw him standing just off the curb, in the street.

"I keep a low profile," he said, climbing into the front seat, directing me down an alley to park in back of his house. "I live in the basement of 922, and the house is empty, so you probably can't see the numbers in the dark."

"I didn't even see the house."

"It's boarded up," he said.

I followed him through the back door and down a long, damp corridor smelling of rodents.

He had lit candles.

"So hello," he said softly.

We were standing face-to-face, and I thought he was going to kiss me then in the dank, subterranean apartment, the light from the candles swimming across our bodies.

He poured red wine in a paper cup and handed it to me.

"You are probably wondering why I live in this hellhole."

"I sort of imagined you hiding out like this," I said.

In my child's mental vision of revolution, it seemed right that Victor should live in this forbidding place, in the basement of a changing neighborhood, more dangerous than not, with an abandoned house above him.

I loved the squalor of his apartment, his furtive life, his mercurial, undependable temperament.

That was what Steven would have loved. Or so I thought.

And suddenly I was imagining myself his chosen accomplice.

For those few weeks that Victor Duarte was the center of my life, he was the closest thing to blind faith I had known since I was young, walking the New York City streets of the Upper West Side with Steven.

"I'm a squatter," he said.

We had sat down on a hard piece of furniture, either a futon or a very low couch. There wasn't enough light from the candles to see. I settled back against the wall.

"I need to be undercover, so I move from place to place. Squatting. You understand?"

I drew my legs up under my chin.

"I looked for you on the Web site for DTT."

"And you didn't find me."

"Isn't DTT the group you belong to?"

"I don't belong," he said. "I work for them, but it's important that no one in the government knows who I am, so I belong to nothing."

"I like that," I said. "A lone bandit."

"Not exactly a bandit," he said quietly.

My hand had fallen against his so that the soft parts of our palms were touching. I sat very still.

"I look for people. That's my night job," he said. "We're actually looking for people considered subversive to freedom. Enemies."

"Like Benjamin?"

"We'll find out." He ran his finger lightly across my palm. "We protect the little people like you and me," he said.

I looked at Victor's face, the bones accentuated by candlelight and shadow, and I thought he was astonishing and brave and true, that I was on the way to being with him.

"Would you like me to sing you the melodies?" I asked, taking Benjamin's letter and my own with Milo's composition out of the backpack.

"I'd like that very much."

In the dim, flickering light, I tried to focus on the score. And then from memory hummed Benjamin's Prelude.

"Nice," he said when I had finished humming.

"Romantic?"

He laughed. "Romantic is the point, isn't it? You make him fall in love with you. That's the plan."

I slid down the wall, moved my body closer to his, my arm falling across his stomach. He straightened and pulled away.

"No, Claire," he said quietly, the heat of his breath warming my neck.

"Why?" I asked.

"We can't be together now. It's not a good idea until this mission is done."

I sat up on my knees. "I misunderstood," I said. "I thought you had something else in mind."

"You didn't misunderstand. You understood exactly. We just have to wait."

In my imagining of that night, late, late, after we had been together, shared a glass of wine, I had planned to give him Steven's shirt.

He put his hand briefly on my knee. "Read me your new letter to Benjamin."

"I can't." I folded the letter, stuffed it in the envelope and put it in the pocket of my backpack. It was nearly midnight, and I was feeling breathless and sick to my stomach, embarrassed to have assumed the wrong relationship with Victor Duarte. I wanted to leave. "I have to go home."

"I'll walk you to the car."

I unzipped my backpack and pulled out Steven's debate-team shirt. "I've brought you something."

I couldn't see Victor's face exactly, but what I did see of it—his glittery-marble eyes, his Roman nose, the outline of a square jaw—is locked in memory. Even now I'm able to reproduce the picture of him in my mind.

He took off his own shirt, burrowed his face in Steven's tee as if he were smelling it, put it over his head, his arms in the sleeves, and what I saw of him in the dim light of the basement room was wild-eyed joy.

He threw back his shoulders, pushed out his chest, his chin tucked like a boxer's.

"Now I'm Steven Frayn," he said.

4

When Eva phoned, I was in Steven's bedroom packing his clothes in an old suitcase that had belonged to my father. Faith called from the kitchen.

"I can't talk," I said, without opening the door.

Faith came in anyway. "Eva says she hasn't talked to you in over a week, that she's phoned several times and you don't return her calls."

"I don't *feel* like talking to Eva."

I took another shirt out of the bureau and put it in the suitcase, my back to Faith, waiting to turn around until she left the room and closed the door.

It had been four days since the night I'd gone to Victor's apartment on Capitol Hill. I'd called his cell phone maybe thirty times, listened to the automatic voice: *"Please leave a message at the tone."*

Sometimes I'd hang up, sometimes I'd leave a message. Twice I'd gone to the house on Thirteenth Street, the first time at dusk, driving into the alley where the entrance to the apartment was located, knocking on the door, but no one answered.

Perhaps he was still at his engineering job.

When I turned to get back into the car, a man with his head down was rummaging in the trash, a young man in baggy pants who raised his head when he heard the car door open.

"Girl!" he said, and I recognized the rolling voice. "Why, how-de-do-de-do to you."

I drove away without acknowledging we'd ever seen each other before.

The next day, a Saturday, I went back to Capitol Hill, arriving early, before eight, thinking surely I'd find Victor still at home. But he didn't answer when I knocked at the back door.

In daylight I could peer into the ground-level windows just enough to see the futon where we had sat, an empty bottle of wine on a table with papers spread around, as if he'd been working when he got a call. A rat was helping himself to an open box of doughnuts left on the futon.

In daylight I could assess the neighborhood, which was mixed—several houses boarded up, others restored or in the process of being restored. A neighborhood, in spite of 9/11 and its proximity to the United States Capitol, becoming something new and better.

Steven must have known this place, I thought. He must have known the basements of houses where I imagined him sitting around a table with other revolutionaries, smoking cigarettes and drinking beer, making plans.

A company of brave hearts like the ones Steven had admired in the eighties in Eastern Europe, who hid in such places as these planning velvet revolutions, the end of Soviet control.

My mother would be proud to know what I was learning about Steven.

I finished packing some of Steven's clothes—the blue dress shirt, which looked wonderful with his dark skin; his favorite jeans, worn low on his hips with an old belt from Chile that had belonged to my mother's father. I wondered if his pants would fit Victor, who was heavier than Steven had been, maybe taller.

I shut the suitcase, went out the back door to the garden, where my cell phone had better reception, and dialed.

"Hello," I said. "I've just packed up some of Steven's clothes for you, since they'll probably fit, and I'll drop them off between the screen door and the front door of 922. Please let me know if you get them. Love, Claire."

Love, Claire. Provocative. I liked that.

Faith was at the table in the kitchen reading the arts section of the *New York Times*. She didn't look up.

"Have you heard from Julia?" I asked, planning to make casual conversation.

"She calls."

"Often?"

"Every day."

"And she's okay?"

"Of course she's not okay. She calls to check on you and David."

I opened the cupboard and took out a box of gingersnaps. For the last week, I had been living on a diet of gingersnaps and cottage cheese.

"She doesn't call me," I said.

"She can't bear to hear in your voice how much you've changed."

"Changed?"

Faith looked up from the paper.

"I'm headed to the lab to meet some students." I slipped my cell phone into the pocket of Lisha's jeans, wearing only *her* clothes lately, and picked up the suitcase. "Just in case my father asks where I am."

Bernard was in the living room with Milo when I walked through, and he got up, following me to the front door.

"Are you leaving forever?" he asked.

"No, Bernard. I'm taking this suitcase full of papers to the lab to work with some summer-school students."

"I don't think it's full of papers," he said. "I think the suitcase is full of Steven's clothes. I was watching from the garden as you packed them."

"Good for you, Bernard."

And I closed the front door, went down the path to the driveway and climbed into Steven's car.

5

The next afternoon, when I came home from school with my letter from Benjamin, Milo was polishing the piano.

Dear Sophia,

Take this letter with a grain of salt. It's very late at night, my work in advanced composition is going poorly, and this studio apartment on a windy, rainy Michigan night is a lonely place to be.

I'm looking for a pen pal.

I've never had a pen pal, but one summer, after my mother died, I discovered a cache of letters in a shoe box in her closet, sweet letters she had written to me while I was probably sleeping in the next room. When I was about ten or eleven, but still a boy, and she'd been dead five years, I answered every letter she had written in my Catholic-schoolboy script.

"Dear Mama," I wrote, "signed Benjamin, your own son," and I put my letters in the shoe box with hers.

PRELUDE II: TO MY PEN PAL

P.S. I'm coming to Washington on August 15 to visit my father, and then I go for a few months to the Czech Republic to study composition with a master teacher. Maybe we'll meet in Washington?

Yours, Benjamin

August 15, I thought. On August 15, I would go to a restaurant and wait in a booth for Benjamin Reed to arrive from Michigan. He'd be surprised to see how tall and thin I am. Already he would have fallen in love with me. My mind rushed ahead to calling V, later that night, after dinner, so I could catch him as he left work.

"Victor?" I'd begin, waiting in silence for his full attention. "Benjamin Reed is coming to Washington on August fifteenth."

"Why do you cut the musical score out of the letter?" Milo was asking as he sat down to play, with the score of Prelude II propped on the piano. "I want to read the whole letter."

"You've never shown me any of your love letters," I said, moving next to him on the bench.

"I don't have any," he said. "I'm in love with my piano, and I have *your* love affair vicariously, so here it goes."

Benjamin's new song was fast and snappy. A nervous, syncopated, high-spirited melody.

"Dazzling," Milo said. "The boy's a goner. Mad for you, Claire."

"He's never even seen me."

"Well, won't he be surprised to find such a beauty at the other end of these songs!"

"He'll be especially surprised to discover his love affair is actually with you," I said.

"Surprised and delighted," Milo agreed.

In the kitchen my father was making tea.

"Should I tell David what we're doing?" Milo asked when we heard my father walking through the hall. "I think he'd be very pleased."

"I'm not ready to tell him," I said as my father came into the living room and leaned against the wall just beyond the piano.

"Was that your composition, Milo?" my father asked.

"More or less," Milo said when he had finished playing. "What do you think?"

"I think I've changed my mind about the piano," my father said. "It's turning out I don't want so much silence after all."

Milo jabbed me gently in the ribs. "See?" he said when my father left the room.

"The piano is working," I said. "You said it would, and it does."

"David likes it. He likes it." Milo ran his fingers down the piano keys. "I knew he would. Eventually he would."

He grabbed my wrist, swinging my arm in the air.

"So now we write an answer to Prelude II, a perfectly beautiful answer to this dumbstruck, lovesick composer."

"Something happy, sort of like falling in love, your feet off the ground, spinning in the air. That kind of song," I said.

"No Eros?"

"I didn't hear Eros in his song to me, but what do I know?"

"It's all in the way you hear it. If you don't hear something, then it isn't there for you. For me, sex is in these melodies, but I'm sixty, and all I have is memory and little of it."

"Then no Eros.

"You want to be an old-fashioned girl but maybe a little co-quette, yes?"

"Coquette is perfect."

I was bemused by my detachment in this adventure. It wasn't even detachment, more like a transformation or adaptation to a new environment, and I was in the process of physically accommodating. I had lost an attachment to my own self. I could do that at the time. I could be Sophia Lupe and believe I was falling in love with this composer who might be implicated in my brother's death.

None of the usual rules applied to what was happening to me.

In the process of becoming someone different, I had been cast adrift. Until this moment I'd been incapable of imagining beyond an immutable self, my constant companion until Steven's death.

My father had finished restoring the left wing of the airplane, and there was a strong smell of trapped chemicals in the hangar. I left the door open.

"Hi," I said.

"I haven't seen you for days."

"I've been busy at the lab, with a lot of work to do at night," I said.

"Missing dinner? You're getting too thin, Claire."

"I'm not trying to miss dinner."

"Tonight Lisha's coming over and Julia will be home."

"For good?

"For dinner."

"So you actually talk to Julia on the phone."

"Several times a day, we talk."

"Then there's hardly a reason for her to have moved into the glass factory, is there?"

"She *had* to move."

"*Had* to move?"

I was standing next to him while he continued gluing something on the wing.

"It's not forever. Nothing is forever," he said.

"I'm learning that."

There was a sharp edge of cruelty to everything I said lately. I could hear it in the tone of my voice with my father, who seemed barely able to get up in the morning, immobilized by everything but the tedium of gluing back together his old airplane.

"It's important to me for you to be at dinner tonight," my father was saying. "I'm asking you to come.

"Okay," I said brusquely. "I understand."

I didn't say I would be there.

I was impatient with him. It annoyed me, all the fussing over an old airplane, the smell of glue, the way he disappeared into himself. Even his body was diminishing.

"Is that all you need from me?" I asked. "I'm a little late, and I've got to go."

He leaned down under the wing of the plane, adjusting a small piece of metal.

"I've actually got to make a call," I said.

He followed me into the garden. "Claire?"

I stopped.

"I know it's not my business, but Julia thinks you've met someone?"

"I haven't *met* anyone," I said, pulling the cell phone out of the pocket of Lisha's tight jean skirt. "But Julia's right. It's not your business."

I walked across the street to call Victor, past the Denvers' house, hoping no one at home would take an interest.

"August fifteenth," I said when Victor's voice mail answered. "And then he leaves the country for a few months."

Victor called back before I even got to our side of the street.

"Café Rouge," he said. "Seven-thirty."

6

There'd been an orange alert that morning, and the streets were empty and full of police. *"Biochemical waste found on the steps of the Capitol,"* flashed on the news every few minutes. *"Don't drink the water from the tap."* We had not been drinking tap water in Washington for years—dangerous levels of lead, bacteria. Pregnant mothers filling up on the required eight glasses of water a day formed protest groups when they discovered they'd been responsible for passing dangerous levels of lead into their unborn babies from the tap. Every front porch in our neighborhood was lined with bottles of spring water.

There were often alerts in Washington, usually orange or yellow, very occasionally red, and people would go home, sometimes walking three or four miles to avoid the subway. They'd leave their offices, call their families on the cell phones they always carried, shut the front doors to their houses, pull down the blinds. The television was on in many homes even in the day during an alert.

We paid attention to orange.

Driving downtown, I was conscious of a solitary man walking the empty Connecticut Avenue just before rush hour, his head bobbing back and forth, checking the avenue. I was alert to trouble, too, although none of us in the Frayn family was actually afraid when the warnings came. The worst had already happened to us.

I did find myself thinking of my family with a sudden wave of loneliness—Julia home for the first time in weeks, talking and talking. Lisha, contained in the glass jar of her small body, picking at her food.

Driving Connecticut Avenue to Foggy Bottom, I rehearsed what to say to Victor. He'd be at the back of the café, his head against the wall, tapping the table with a pencil or his finger—something he always did, a sign of impatience or irritation or worry. I'd weave through the tables glancing at the other customers as if I were looking for friends, an expression of extended boredom on my face.

But boredom was not what I was feeling. I was on a balance beam between laughter and tears, uncontrollable laughter gathering in my throat. It was clear to me with an approaching hysteria that on August 15—soon, very soon, a matter of weeks—Victor and I would deliver my brother's murderer to the law.

The mind, even the rational mind, is a curious thing, the way it grips the tracks once it's on a course. I think I understand now how a soldier in a war zone, an ordinary boy from a loving family, can fall into step and discover in himself the capacity to kill.

Victor was sitting in the booth where we'd first met, wearing Steven's blue shirt and jeans. He seemed especially glad to see me.

"Hello," I said, heat rising in my body.

He reached over, took my chin in his hand and kissed me on the lips.

It was the first time he had kissed me.

"Now we order champagne."

He motioned to a waiter carrying a tray of beers and chips.

"Champagne?" he asked.

"No champagne here, buddy," the waiter said. "Beer or wine."

"Wine?" He looked at me.

"White," I said.

He toasted me when the waiter brought the wines. "A celebration in anticipation of our August fifteenth victory." He downed his wine in a swallow. "So we're ready for action."

"Do you know what plans we'll have when Benjamin comes?" I asked.

"For now the plans are up to you."

"It's a long time to keep these songs going back and forth," I said.

"But you've done it brilliantly."

His chest was broader than Steven's had been, so the buttons on my brother's blue shirt were pulled, his chest fuzzy like Steven's, with thick, curly hair, and his arms dark with black bristles. It gave me a chill to see him in my brother's clothes, as if I'd been caught in something shameful. If Julia knew I had taken them, she would kill me.

He reached over, taking Milo's musical score from my hand. "This sappy letter from him is more than I could have hoped for," he said. "How's this music?"

"Sort of wild and exciting. Jumpy music. My uncle Milo says it's excellent."

"We'll play the game by ear," he said, amused at himself. "Benjamin's hooked—that's clear—and when he does arrive in Washington, you'll figure a way to meet him."

He rolled over the words in an easy fashion, but I was sure his body, like mine, was an explosive.

"This is how I see things happening for the next few weeks." He passed the letter back to me and, leaning across the table, pressed my palms together between his hands. "You keep these love songs going on with the two of you so he'll be urgent to see you when he gets here."

I could tell he was looking at me, but my head was down, watching his hands around mine, conscious of his rapid breathing.

An internal disturbance, like a sudden arrhythmia, upset my equilibrium, passed through my skin with the sizzle of an electric current. I felt myself slipping away.

"And you'll arrange to meet as soon as he arrives, say for coffee, maybe even dinner. Suggest Capitol Hill. It's near his father's house."

Victor looked across the room, and I followed his eyes, which were fixed on an abstract painting, squiggly red and black worms crawling across the canvas hanging on the wall just to the right of me.

"So you'll call and tell me where and when you're meeting him," he said. "And I'll appear. Just a coincidence, he'll think. I'll be a friend coming into the restaurant, stopping to say, 'Oh, hello, Sophia.' You'll introduce us, say I'm an engineer, nothing about Steven, and then you'll excuse yourself and leave me at the table with Benjamin while you go to the bathroom."

"What will you say to him?" I asked.

"I'll shoot the breeze for a while, and if you stay away five to ten minutes, no longer, that will give me the time to ask significant questions."

"Like what kinds of questions?" I asked, a flicker of doubt in Victor, rising, catching in my throat.

"I'm good at leading questions, searching for the answer I need to hear. That's the kind of work I do for DTT."

"And then we'll turn him in, yes?"

At one moment he was leaning toward me, my hands in his, and then he dropped my hands, pushing away from the table, on his face a look of such blackness that it spread across the table, as if a boulder had fallen between us, and for the first time since I met him that morning in the library, I was uneasy.

"We *will* turn him in, won't we? Isn't that what you said?"

He seemed not to be listening, not to hear me, and I reached over, grabbed his arm.

"V?" I started to get up.

Something was happening in my body, like a heart attack, but it wasn't a heart attack. My mouth was dry, my heart beating in my throat, a sense of overwhelming doom sweeping over me as if I were going to die.

In the artificial yellow light shining through the green shades of the fixtures at Café Rouge, Victor's face was reptilian, his eyes cold and wet, disappearing into his head, and I stood up, my legs shaky.

"I'm feeling sick," I said.

In the ladies' room, I splashed cold water on my face and checked the mirror. I was pale, my pupils dilated, sandpaper in my throat. I leaned against the wall next to the towel dispenser, closing my eyes.

I heard the door open, footsteps across the tile floor.

A woman who had been in one of the stalls touched my arm.

"Are you okay?" she asked.

"I don't know," I said, opening my eyes. "I don't feel very well."

I had seen this woman the first time I'd met Victor. She'd been sitting at a round table in the middle of the room, her back to us. What I remembered especially was her steel-gray hair, long enough to sit on. They were friends, Victor had told me. Her name was Rosie, and he had met her at DTT, and they'd been having coffee at the long table at Café Rouge the first time he'd seen Steven.

She had an angular face and violet eyes so close together she appeared cross-eyed, like the blue point Siamese cat Milo had brought with him when he moved in.

"Have I seen you before?" She opened her bag, reached in and pulled out a tin of aspirin and some Tums. "I have seen you." She handed me the pills, reaching into her bag again. "Here's Valium . . . well, something like Valium. You seem a little slippery in the eyes."

I put the Valium in the pocket of my jacket.

"I've seen *you*," I said, taking deep breaths. "*Your* name is Rosie."

"Vanessa," she said. "Your face is familiar, but I don't think we've met."

She had taken out a comb and was running it through the long strands of gray hair.

"You're here with that good looking stocky guy who I used to see a lot. I come to the Café Rouge pretty much every night, but I don't know his name."

She leaned over the sink checking a blemish on her forehead.

"Victor," I said, my mind cranking slowly through the contradictory news I was getting.

Victor had lied to me. This woman was not Rosie. They were not friends. She didn't even know him, except by sight. And why would he bother to lie? I asked myself.

What did it matter to me, the identity of a stranger?

"His name is Victor Duarte," I said.

"I wouldn't have thought he was a Victor. I thought of him as Bud. Cliff. Sonny. Names like that."

The woman was wetting her comb.

"He has such large hands," she said, combing her bangs straight down on her forehead. "I remember he used to come here a lot with that law student who was killed in April. And after that he stopped coming until I saw him here with you. Do you remember the law student?"

She turned with her back the mirror.

"He was assassinated," she said. "At least that's what they called it in the newspaper." She put her makeup back in her purse, took out a small pack of sugar, opened it and sprinkled it on her tongue. "Energy!"

I leaned against the wall. It crossed my mind that I was in the process of dying, that some chemical change was taking place and my body was floating downstream, out of my control.

There was something I needed to ask her, but already I knew the answer.

"Are you a member of DTT?"

I was running out of air.

"DTT." She shook her head. "I've never heard of it."

I felt myself sinking to the ground. The next thing I remember, the door to the bathroom was propped open and I was lying on the floor and the gray-haired woman was holding a small paper bag over my mouth and nose.

"You hyperventilated," Victor said, walking to my car with me. "Tension, the woman in the bathroom told me. She said she gave you a Valium and you put it in your pocket."

"I don't want a Valium."

"Are you okay to drive home?"

"Fine," I said. "The woman's name is Vanessa."

"Rosie," Victor said firmly. "Rosie St. John. I've known her forever."

An injured animal responds to danger with a rush of adrenaline and is capable of enormous strength, which can propel him to safety if he doesn't die of the injury.

Random incidentals from Biology I, sometimes whole sentences pinned to a single moment, ran through my mind that summer.

"No Valium. I'll be fine," I said.

We walked up the steps to the parking garage, his arm around my waist. I was aware of an accumulating fear, and I wanted to get home.

He opened the door to the car, and I got in, and he climbed into the passenger seat, folding his arms across his chest.

"Drop me at the Foggy Bottom Metro if you feel okay to drive home," he said.

I turned the key in the ignition.

I could feel him looking at me as I paid the ticket and pulled onto Twenty-first Street. I couldn't see his expression, didn't have a sense of how he saw me now and whether he sensed what had just happened between us, whether it mattered.

"I have evidence that Benjamin killed your brother, and he may even have been acting on orders. I know I can ask him the kinds of questions that will force him inadvertently to tell the truth."

"And then we'll go to the police?" I asked.

"One thing at a time."

"I thought the whole point was to turn him in."

"Once we *know* he did it," Victor said. "We can't jump to conclusions."

"But as soon as we know?"

"We'll call the police," he said. "Your role has been as a decoy, like one of those wooden ducks hunters put in the water to lure the real ducks, and you've done beautifully."

I didn't react. I have always been slow to react, by nature porous, like a sponge, and it wasn't until much later that I began to understand the full measure of what I had agreed to do, of what I had done.

Victor got out of the car and leaned in the open window on my side, his hand on my arm.

"Drive safely," he said.

Everyone was in bed when I got home, except my father, who was in the hangar. My mother's car was gone, so she must have returned to the glass factory after dinner. I opened the fridge, took out the remains of a roasted chicken and pulled off pieces of white meat, leaning against the kitchen sink, eating out of weakness, not hunger. I took a bunch of grapes, saltines and a glass of wine back to Steven's room.

In bed I turned out the light and lay awake. A full moon over the trees in the backyard lit the shadeless room. Sometime after midnight the light in the hangar went out, so my father must have gone to sleep.

I got out of bed, turned on the light, took some paper and a pen out of Steven's desk drawer and climbed back under the sheets, propped by pillows.

Dear Steven,

Today is July 12. You've been dead three months, and it never occurred to me until today that I could write to you. It's not a question now of whether you read what I have written but of whether I write it in the first place.

I have these questions:

Did you ever know a man called Victor Duarte?

Were you friends?

Were you with HIM when you used to disappear?

Did you ever meet Benjamin Reed?

Do you have any idea who killed you?

I wanted to think your death was an accident, although there is evidence now that it was not. Someone knew where we lived and came with the blue Department of Justice flag the night before you died.

All of my love forever, C

P.S. I don't expect to hear from you, but I suppose I wouldn't be writing if I didn't believe that something could materialize by way of truth. A long time ago, we had a funny talk about the fearless birds in the Galápagos, and remembering it tonight, I decided to write.

I must have fallen asleep just as I finished the letter. When I woke up, I was still sitting against a mound of pillows, the lamp on beside my bed, my letter to Steven facedown on my stomach.

THE LIFEGUARD CHAIR

The first time we went to the Galápagos, I remember in particular the birds. Lying on my back, the sun high overhead, I rested my head on Steven's leg. The birds were all over me, nibbling at my lips, sitting on my shoulder, examining strands of my hair, languishing on my stomach cleaning their wings.

"Why don't they fly away like normal birds?" I asked my father.

"Because they have no reason to be afraid of us," he'd replied. "There are no predators here."

Steven, bored with the long boat trip and the turtles and the endless walks with guides and their tedious information, was outraged at the birds.

"I want to force them to be afraid of me," he said.

"You can do that if it's important to you," my father replied. "You can easily prove to them that you're the enemy, and they'll stay away from you."

This morning, a Tuesday, my seventeenth birthday, and Steven has forgotten to say happy birthday, although it's already seven o'clock and he is leaving for university. He is standing by the door ready to go, his lacrosse stick and helmet slung over his shoulders. Surely his mind is on a woman at school.

"Remember the Galápagos?" I ask, hoping to delay him.

Steven smiles, that amazing smile, full of light, as if it has been ignited from within.

"Those idiot birds drove me crazy," he says.

He struggles through the back door with all of his equipment and his backpack, and just before he closes it, he leans his head in.

"Happy birthday, gorgeous."

C.F., age 17

Blue-footed Booby, Galápagos

VII.

SYMBIOSIS

I

July 21

Dear Sophia,

I'm a reasonable man. A little abstracted and obssessional. My hair too long, my jeans threadbare, my living room floor a closet for the number of clothes I have dropped on there.

But my brain is arranged in file cabinets, the drawers marked for every occasion except this one.

Another thing. I'm the only son of a conservative politician from a small town in the Midwest, and I learned early with such a legacy to defend my heart.

This epistolary folly is insane, I tell myself.

And then I sit down at the piano to compose a sonata for advanced composition, and what comes to mind?

PUT ON YOUR HIGH HEELS, BABY, AND DANCE OVER HERE TO ME

July 26

Dear Sophia,

Your brother sounds amazing, and it's a compliment to look like him, if only in a foggy photo in the daily press. But I'm not political or particularly courageous or outspoken, so I'm afraid that trying to BE your brother will turn out a disastrous failure.

What I am is an obsessed piano player with good hands and enough concentration and neurosis and desire to be a musician, maybe a composer.

AND I'm a bit of nerd, like my father.

Still there?

I just got "Hey, Mister, Sing A Long" from you. Pure song and so funny.

So "Here's looking at you!" AND . . .

HANGING BY MY KNEES

I arrive in the flesh at 3:15, Northwest Airlines, on the fifteenth of August. I don't expect you to meet the plane, but I'll be wearing eggshells in case you do.

"I love it," Milo said, playing "Hanging by My Knees." "Don't you love it?"

The music was fast and dramatic, capped by a final run over the keys with the backs of his fingers. Milo played it again and again.

"Crazy," Milo said. "Completely wonderfully crazy and daring. I am in love with this composer, and you should be, too."

It was a Saturday, and my father was in the kitchen with Julia, who had moved home until she got over the cold she caught sleeping in a draft at the glass factory.

"It's a temporary visitation," she said. "Not to be confused with the word 'return.' "

The FBI had stopped by in the morning with more questions, hoping for a "breakthrough" clue, as Agent Burns said, but I wasn't listening, sidelined by my own problems. At one point I did hear them ask my father the specific circumstances surrounding his departure from NIH. I listened for that answer.

"What difference does it make?" my father asked.

"Did your leaving have anything to do with the boy who wanted you to adopt him?"

"I can't answer that," he said initially.

But he sat in a loaded silence, pressing the ends of his fingers in the shape of a diamond, considering what he might say.

The agents waited, shifting on the rush seats of our hard-back chairs, trying to get comfortable, their arms resting on the table. I was at the end of the table, watching my mother rattle around the sink doing the dishes.

"Are you going to say something, David?"

Finally she turned off the water and sat down beside my father, a wet dish towel over her shoulder, and her presence, her noisy presence, was of some comfort to him.

"I don't know if this answers your question," he began. "But I will tell you what went on with me."

He tipped his chair back, pushed his hands into the pockets of his pants.

"Originally I had in mind to work with patients. It was why I wanted to be a doctor in the first place, the only reason. But I chose to work in the lab, because—and I know this makes no sense—I was afraid I wouldn't be successful helping the sick. That I could do harm."

"Do no harm," Julia interceded, repeating the Hippocratic oath.

"I couldn't save any of the patients under my charge at NIH. Not personally. Maybe the research I was involved with will eventually make a difference in some lives," he said. "But not personally, and that was too difficult for me."

He got up to leave the room, probably embarrassed, certainly exposed, nonconfessional by nature. I couldn't look at him. He was standing at the door to the hall.

"I don't know why I said that just now," he said. "What did you ask me? Why did I leave NIH?" He shook his head. "It's no one's business but my own."

I had my father's ability to fly at such a high altitude above my life that what I didn't see—and it was easy for me to hide out from myself—had no viable existence.

Now I lay awake nights watching the coming of dawn, replaying the scene in the bathroom with Vanessa/Rosie St. John at the Café Rouge in the bright room of my mind.

What was Steven doing with Victor, I wondered, and how often did they see each other, and why? What did I really know about my brother?

Milo and I spent every evening at the piano, Milo composing with me beside him, listening until I knew the music well enough to hear it in my head without the piano. There was a sense of safety about those hours together, Bernard on the couch behind us, clapping when the music was finished, mumbling encouragement, telling me I was turning into an excellent composer, although I never once made up a melody.

At some point in early August, I stopped responding to Benjamin's letters with anything more than music. My early letters had been full of the life of Sophia Lupe, but she was slipping away, and I had no particular desire to retrieve her. Without Sophia I had nothing to say to Benjamin, nothing I could say except these songs.

My family was curious about the music. They'd stop by the door to the living room or sit with Bernard, who was always there when Milo was playing, and then they'd leave without a comment. I'm sure they were glad that I was home at night, looking like myself since Lisha had taken her clothes back and left for Germany with her parents, to recover.

I was beginning to take an interest in things again. Faith had purchased some praying mantises from Gray's Flower Center on Old Georgetown Road to protect the flower bed she'd planted that summer in front of the house. They came in a small bag, hundreds of them, hatched and frozen and when she scattered the babies in the garden in early June, many of them grew to adulthood and filled the front yard with praying mantises feeding on insects damaging to plants.

One afternoon before dinner, I found myself on my hands and knees watching their delicate heads arched against the hydrangea leaves in an attitude of prayer.

Victor called, but only in the evening when my phone was turned off so he could leave a message. He had taken to calling me his "lucky charm." Every message began, *"Is this my lucky charm?"* And each time I heard these words in his distinctive voice, I felt a panic coming on.

The messages were brief—*"I'm here or there,"* he'd say. *"Working for DTT tonight." "Moving to a new place soon, but maybe not until September."* Street noises in the background, the scream of sirens. *"Heading to a meeting with my DTT buddies."*

I deleted his messages, not wishing to play them over and over as I did when I was attached to his voice, listening for signs of affection in the tone.

Something like faith had come unraveled, and even his face or the sound of his voice had taken on a different texture. But I was trapped, and I put Victor Duarte out of mind whenever I could.

Something was happening to me with Benjamin.

August 3

Dear Sophia,

In answer to your questions:

1. *The hardest thing in my life? No contest. Losing my mother, although I didn't know it at the time. It has defined me.*

2. *My father? My father and I are not alike, which we accommodate in a formal way but with affection. I know he loves me, but often when we're together, especially now I'm older, we sit in front of the television watching the news in pained silence. The spirit ignited in him by my mother died with her. When you are young and someone you love dies young, she becomes a perfect work of art.*

3. *My biggest success? I hope it hasn't happened yet.*

4. *My biggest failure? The one that stays out of a long list of unkindnesses and temper tantrums and convenient lies is permanent, like a birthmark, which I also have in the shape of a small black pear on my shoulder. When I was in sixth grade, a new boy came to school whose mother had just died, and he had no father. Maybe because I was the only kid in the class whose mother had also died, and I wanted no competition in suffering, I took off after him with a group of other boys, and we taunted him until he stopped coming to school.*

5. *Item #4 is my shame, and I can't even believe I'm writing it down for you to read. You seem to be a lovely, generous, sweet woman and by now have changed your mind about me and will not be writing back.*

6. *Love in my life? NA.*

On another note:

DELPHINIUM EVENINGS

Milo played the long lyrical passages of "Delphinium Evenings," moving his body into the notes with exaggerated emotion.

"Beautiful, yes?" he asked.

We were alone in the living room, except for Bernard sitting quietly on the couch.

"Beautiful," I agreed.

He stood, brushed off his trousers and reached out his arms to me.

"Would you like to dance?"

"It would be a pleasure," I said.

I moved into the circle of his arms. Milo, for all his awkwardness, was a graceful dancer.

"Can you hear the music?" he asked.

"In my head."

My parents were in the kitchen and must have seen us dancing, and I wondered what they were possibly thinking. How unlikely and strange this music between Uncle Milo and me must seem to them, how out of the ordinary for a man like Milo and a girl like me.

"Can you write one more song for me?" I asked him after we had danced. "The last song before he comes."

"Of course, of course. Certainly, no question."

"I want it to be about the birth of butterflies," I said.

"Why not?" Milo's hands fluttered above the keys, thinking. "If you'll tell him you're a biologist and not a composer."

I laughed. "Maybe I will if the occasion arises."

I got up from the piano bench so Milo could compose alone, as he preferred to do.

"Claire?" he called as I was leaving the living room. "Can we tell your father about the composer when he arrives from Michigan?"

"If he comes," I said.

"Oh, he'll come. He's probably on his way from Michigan now."

2

Benjamin Reed arrived in Washington from Detroit three hours late, just before 6:00 P.M. on August 15. The weather was stormy from Chicago to the Atlantic, according to the ticket agent at Northwest Airlines with whom I spoke.

I had been lying on Steven's bed all day, pretending to read, on break between summer sessions from my job in the biology lab.

In the kitchen my parents worked on a list of acquaintances from Steven's past for the FBI. They had been given old class lists from our elementary school and junior high and high school. My father had paid very little attention to the names or faces of Steven's friends, but Julia had a remarkable memory and could describe the friends and their parents and situations and the peculiarities of people like Adele

Stockman, the mother of Rufus, who came to the first PTA meeting when Steven was in third grade wearing a red halter top and short shorts.

Julia had left her home at the glass factory in early June, intending to return when she felt better. But her cold dragged on, and her weariness accentuated the sadness, and so she took a leave of absence until the fall.

All day they sat in the kitchen, eating sourdough bread and olives, working on their lists. Only at night, with the prospect of sharing the double bed they'd always shared, did my father return to the hangar to work and then to sleep.

Milo was putting together a selection of his own compositions, mainly the love songs between Benjamin and me, calling it Preludes to Night Music.

After work Bernard sat on the couch in the living room, leafing through newsmagazines, looking at the photographs and listening to Milo.

Faith was beginning to like her new job at the Commerce Department. She even mentioned having lunch with Charles Reed, and I wanted to ask her about it, but of course I couldn't. One morning at breakfast, she asked me, in such a way that I could tell she'd been worrying about it, if I had told Steven that she'd been fired.

"I didn't want to be the one to tell him," I said. "I thought he'd find out at dinner that night."

She was genuinely relieved and took my hand and kissed my fingers.

We held on to small threads.

A sense of the normal was returning to our lives. At least to my family's life.

I was skipping across a minefield. No predicting where my foot might fall.

That morning I'd sat at Steven's desk trying to discover what had happened to me by filling in the days on his calendar from April 4 through the middle of August. I marked the days in May and June I'd been with Victor Duarte in red ink and the musical correspondence with Benjamin in blue, and in those seventy days between early May and mid-August, I could see a graph, as if it were the angled lines of a heart monitor, of what had begun to feel like insanity.

In Benjamin's last song, he had added a postscript: *"Trocadero's at 23rd and S at 10 the evening August 15."*

I looked up Trocadero's in the phone book and drove by to check it out. It was a small, intimate place with a bar on the first floor, dining room on the second, low lights and white tablecloths, vases of tulips. I could imagine us there.

At noon on August 15, Victor called my cell phone.

"I thought I would have heard from you by now," he said. "Any word?"

"No word," I said.

"Can you meet tonight?"

"With him?"

"With me."

"I don't know," I said.

I didn't have a plan from one hour to the next, hoping some sense of order might surface after I met Benjamin.

"I'll call you back when I know what I'm doing."

I clicked off the phone and buried my face in a pillow, closing out the light.

Whoever Victor Duarte was, and of that I wasn't sure, I knew that his mission was no longer mine.

I lifted the pillow from my face just as Julia came in, without knocking as usual.

"Eli Trueheart, do you remember?" She stood at the door. "Curly carrot hair, crooked teeth."

"I don't remember Eli Trueheart."

"His parents wouldn't allow him to come over to play at our house."

"What was the matter with our house?" I sat up in bed.

"Nothing was the matter with our house," she said. "The problem was with the Truehearts."

I tried to keep the door to Steven's room closed, but Julia kept arriving with a new possibility for her collection, and gradually I realized I was actually pleased to listen to her accumulating list from the past, relieved to see my parents in the same room together, trying to make sense of our lives without Steven.

Victor called again at three, but I didn't pick up.

"Benjamin is delayed until six because of the weather," the voice mail began. There was a hollow silence, and I was just about to delete the message when Victor's voice, a little desperate, came on again.

"Call me as soon as you can. I have new and important evidence about Steven's death."

I pressed "end" to turn off my cell phone and slipped it into my pocket.

Faith stopped by Steven's room when she got home from work and sat on the end of the bed.

"Milo told me," she said.

It was hot, and her blue linen blouse was wet with perspiration, damp curls framed her face, and she looked as lovely and sweet as I used to think of her.

"He told you about the music?"

"About the young composer."

I blushed.

"Milo says he's coming today."

"He hasn't called."

"He will," she said, reaching out for me. "I'm so glad for you, Claire, after the awful year you've had, and I hope it works out."

I wanted to tell her who the young composer was, that he was Charles Reed's son, that I was meeting him at Trocadero's that night and that it wouldn't work out between us. It could never work out.

But I didn't know what was true. Not about Victor Duarte or Benjamin or myself. Especially about myself.

I felt as if I were holding on to the back of an old caboose, which seemed to be stopped in a station but was in fact traveling faster than the speed of sound. If I were to release my grip on the railing, I would catapult into space.

There was no telling if I could survive.

Benjamin called while Faith was still lying on the bed talking about her photographer boyfriend and how she hadn't felt the desire to see him since Steven's death.

"Your phone?" she asked when it rang in the pocket of my pants. "Maybe it's the call."

"Sophia?" he asked when I answered the call.

"Yes, it is," I said, struck by the name Sophia spoken aloud.

"It's so odd to hear your voice after all this time of knowing each other."

"It is." I held the phone tight to my ear.

"I hate to start like this, but I need to cancel tonight so I can be with my father," he said. "Just tonight."

I was relieved. I hadn't figured how I could sustain the charade of Sophia Lupe face-to-face with Benjamin, counting on my instinct. I hadn't even thought what this meeting between us could be, and now I couldn't imagine anything beyond the menace of a slow, linear advance of time.

Maybe by tomorrow Benjamin would have changed his mind, would have reconsidered meeting at all, deciding that direct-mail music was a better way to go.

"Can I call you later?" he was asking. "Maybe after eleven?"

I drew my knees under my chin, avoiding Faith's curious look.

"I'm terrified," he said.

I rolled over onto my stomach and turned the cell off so I wouldn't hear from Victor.

"The composer?" Faith asked.

"He can't see me tonight."

"Men!" Faith got up, smoothed the bedspread. "Julia's made coq au vin, and it smells yummy." She toussled my hair.

After dinner I stayed at the table with my parents, listening as they made their lists. They were working sequentially and had reached seventh and eighth grades at Milton Junior High.

I was mesmerized by the rhythmic sound of their voices, my chin resting on my fist, my eyes slipping into sleep. I no longer felt superior to their task or believed it was futile to go through the names of possible suspects, as I had thought earlier.

Whatever Victor said or wanted me to believe, Benjamin Reed was not responsible for Steven's death. I knew that.

If I were to ask myself now when I knew and how, I might say I began to know while I sat next to Uncle Milo, listening to the songs, and something like a seed took root in me and grew.

But the truth is, I don't know how these things happen. When Steven was murdered, I went from shock to a kind of surreal rationality to terror in a matter of hours.

Then, as I perceived it at the time, I was saved by Victor Duarte's mission of justice.

My mother read the names aloud, reported what she remembered, waited for my father to say, "No, I never heard of that child." And then went on to the next name.

"Beatrice Shoe," my mother was saying. "I remember Beatrice Shoe. She had those breasts in seventh grade and didn't wear a bra."

"Did she have anything to do with Steven?" my father asked, his head resting in his hands. "Otherwise let's move on."

"A crush. She used to call him several times a week. But here is Liza Schmidt, and he broke her heart. That's something."

"I don't think we need to include Liza Schmidt on the FBI list," he said.

"We have to put *someone* on it."

My father checked the list. "We have seven people, and that's plenty," he said.

"For all the years we've lived here? It's nothing," my mother said. "We may as well have been recluses."

"Everyone knew each other in Llangollen, and I don't really remember seven people there, although it's a national pastime in Wales to remember."

"You remember Meryn What's-Her-Name."

My father let that pass.

Milo was calling from the living room for us to listen.

"He's going to play his new CD." Bernard sat down at the table with us.

"He hasn't made a CD," Julia said. "That's insane."

"Hush," Milo called. "Duh-de-duh-DUM. Friends and family and invited guests. Preludes to Night Music, a sonata composed and performed by Miles Augusten Frayn."

I got up in the middle of the recital of Milo's music, which I had already heard over and over, and went into Steven's room to check my messages.

There were two voice mails, one from Eva and the second from Victor Duarte.

"News?" he asked when I called back.

"Nothing," I said.

I had made up my mind to tell him nothing. Nothing about Benjamin. Nothing at all.

"Nothing? What's the matter with the guy? Some kind of wimp?"

"Maybe he isn't going to call, Victor," I said. "He's only here for a short time, and I'm not high on his list of priorities."

"He's going to call," Victor said. "I'm dead certain of that, but if he doesn't do it soon, you'll go over to his father's house and find him." I heard him shuffle papers, clear his throat. "Here. I have the address: 310 A Street SE, just off East Capitol at Third."

I took a deep breath, the air slipping away as it had in the ladies' room of Café Rouge.

"Let's wait until tomorrow," I said.

I lay on the top of the bedspread thinking about Sophia Lupe. For weeks I had had a plan. I'd meet Benjamin in a café. We'd talk about this and that, childhood stories, my brother's death from encephalitis, my Latina family. Fifteen minutes of conversation, no longer. Victor would appear, sit down, engage Benjamin, and I would leave.

Now, thinking of Sophia Lupe, I couldn't imagine sitting at lunch with Benjamin Reed and making her up on the spot. In the last weeks, she had deserted me, and nothing had surfaced to replace the space she'd filled.

I didn't know what Victor had in mind for Benjamin Reed. Only that somewhere along the timeline of revenge, we were supposed to deliver Benjamin to the FBI.

3

My father stopped by my room on his way to the hangar and stuck his head in the door.

"Would you like to talk?" he asked.

"About what?" I asked. It wasn't in his character to probe.

"Just talk," he said. "If you'd like. I'm going to the hangar for the night now."

I waited, watching the light in the hangar, hoping he might turn it off. I had a sense of foreboding and didn't want to know what he had in mind.

But it began to look as if he would wait all night for me to come, so I slipped out the back door and crossed the garden to the hangar.

"I'm glad you're here," he said.

He pulled over a faded deck chair for me to sit, put his feet up on his desk.

"I've been thinking about guilt, so tonight I looked it up in the *Oxford English Dictionary*."

"Why guilt?"

"Because that's how I feel all the time about Steven." He tipped his chair back. "As if I'd had a hand in what happened to him. Remember you told me you were frightened after Steven died."

I twisted in the chair, stretching my legs out in front of me, wondering if I could escape the room without offending him, without having to listen to his confession.

"What the *Oxford* said about 'guilt' is what you'd expect." He was looking out the window into the streetlight above the Denvers' house. "Like culpability, wrongdoing, misconduct, misbehavior, turpitude, transgression, sin, vice, on and on." He turned the shade on the lamp so he was in shadow. "Those don't describe how I feel."

It had become clear since Steven died that my mother was too aggressive in her emotions for the quiet conversations my father needed to have. Her moods pushed him out of the room.

"Guilt, at least the way I'm aware of it, is the loss of control."

He crossed his legs, folded his hands around his knee, and in the light from outside the window, he looked as if his eyes had sunk beneath the surface. "I've lost control."

I started to ask him, What does it matter? The dictionary definition—the semantics of language—this isn't science. Another definition won't alter the way you feel.

But he was struggling, and so I waited, saying nothing as he arranged a conversation in his mind.

"Julia brought up Meryn tonight at dinner," he said. "You remember Meryn, the girl whose picture—"

"I remember."

"It was winter, and we were seventeen, and the Dee was frozen. It seldom froze, too much current, but as we went under the main bridge over the river in Llangollen, the ice broke, and we slipped into the water, and I got out."

"I don't want to know," I said, speaking sweetly but getting up to leave. "You have to understand. It's too much after this year. I begin to believe that everything is an accident, and I don't want to feel that way."

"I want you to understand what I mean about control," he said.

"I do understand about control," I said. "I'm not as innocent as you think I am. Not any longer."

"I'm talking about myself, Claire," he said. "That's why I told you the story."

"I didn't like the story," I said. "It's as if you think of yourself as destructive."

"I do," my father said, getting up, following me to the door, opening it for me to leave.

Back in Steven's room, I couldn't sleep. The light from the hangar spread across the bed, and even with my eyes tight shut, it filtered though the lids. And my eyelids turned into a movie screen with familiar images flashing across the surface—Olivia, my white rat, sitting on her haunches in the garden at night, the pallid bat, Julia's gift from the glass factory on the day that Steven died—again and again a floating picture of my first treasure, the black and white kitten still in the floppy fetal sac, swimming in formaldehyde.

THE LIFEGUARD CHAIR

We just got back from visiting my grandmother Frayn in Llangollen, who is quite old and difficult to understand, not because she's old but because she's Welsh. Mama tells me she may die soon, so I should pay particular attention to what she has to say, because sometime before too long she won't be saying it any longer.

What she had to say to me at this visit for my ninth birthday was about strawberries, which she grows on her farm at the edge of town just above the canal. She sat on the damp ground in her big woolly skirt, pulled me down with her and showed me the strawberries creeping along the ground around the garden fence. She picked one up, put it in the cup of my hand and told me to look at it very carefully.

"You see that mass of tiny black seeds right at the place the skin of the strawberry has been torn by the wire fence it ran into while it was growing."

I did see them.

"And here," she said, "is the tear, which has healed over so you can't see the raw flesh, but you can see that the lovely strawberry has been smart

enough to toughen up her skin with a peppering of seeds in case she runs into another wire fence."

"Can I eat it?" I asked.

"No, love. Don't eat this brave strawberry. Put it in your pocket and keep it to remember."

C.F., age 9

An injured strawberry in my pocket

VIII.

BENJAMIN IN THE FLESH

I

I left a note on the kitchen table:

"Not to worry. He's arrived, and I'll be gone probably all day with him. Claire"

I assumed that Milo would fill in the blanks.

There had been a message from Benjamin the night before:

"Meet me at six A.M. at the front gate to Dumbarton Oaks. Is that too early? I have to be home by noon."

It was dawn when I left the house, the air wild with birdsong, the beginning of a soft summer day. The streets were empty except for an occasional bus, clear all the way down Wisconsin Avenue, mist salting the windshields.

In the rearview mirror, I checked my skin for bloom.

I had to remind myself not to press the accelerator to the floor and fly there.

Benjamin Reed was waiting by his car, leaning against the trunk in khaki shorts and a white T-shirt. He was darker-skinned than I had expected, fine-boned, with a deep dimple on one side of his lips, his hair long and unruly.

I crossed to his side of the street, feeling awkward, off balance, a long-legged goose of a girl.

"Sophia?"

"Hello."

We stood head-to-head.

At some level of consciousness, I must have been aware of the danger of this charade, keeping mental track of the facts I had told him about Sophia Lupe's life so I wouldn't betray my own deceit. I couldn't drop the story of Sophia now, maybe not ever, couldn't possibly tell Benjamin the truth.

Whatever had broken the trust I had in Victor Duarte—Vanessa/Rosie St. John, or Victor's own strangeness, or the songs with Benjamin—as if he were some kind of savior instead of a stranger, the trust was gone as quickly as it had come that evening at the Café Rouge.

Something was the matter with him, and I had enough remaining animal instinct to recognize that now.

In retrospect I have no memory of what electrical current traveled the crossed wires of my brain. Dawn at Dumbarton Oaks with another stranger. I must have put trouble out of my mind, and for that moment I could believe my life no more complicated than this new arrival on my horizon.

"You're tall!" he said with pleasure, as if I had grown especially for him. "You didn't tell me that."

"It's a surprise who I am, isn't it?" I said, slipping my hands into the pockets of my pants. "I could be anyone."

"A mischief maker is what you are." He laughed. "All those songs!"

The gates to the garden were closed—it was too early in the morning for Dumbarton Oaks to open—and I followed Benjamin to a path just to the side of the entrance, lush with the growth of late summer.

"This path goes all the way north, coming out behind the Safeway, parallel to Wisconsin Avenue, and almost no one knows about it except the homeless," he said. "You'll see."

He stopped to look at me.

"You're the perfect height," he said. "And lovely."

I had never been called lovely. My mother said I was beautiful, but "lovely" was a different word, and I liked the sound of it, imagining lovely as deeper than beautiful.

We walked down a steep hill, the roots of trees breaking through along the path obstructing our way so we had to hold on to the branches above us to keep from falling.

The trees were craggy, thick-trunked, pressed together. Pine and beech and oak, a scattering of dogwood, heavy with leaves spreading a green umbrella above us as we made our way deeper into the woods, along a muddy path, the rising sun dappling our hair and arms.

"I thought it would be crazy to meet for coffee the first time," he was calling over his shoulder to me. "Everybody does that. Or drinks in a bar so crowded you can't hear yourself talk."

"I know," I said, dropping down a small hill, walking level with him. "I love that we came here."

"So tell me everything," he said. "Your whole life, from the beginning to now."

Once in junior high, I'd asked Steven what happens the first time when you get together with a girl.

"Sex?" I'd asked.

"Stories," he'd said. "She tells you her story and you tell her yours. And then sex. But the stories have to be worth it."

I wanted to tell Benjamin everything. My own life.

"I'm Claire Frayn," I wanted to say. "Sophia Lupe is a fraud. I, Claire Frayn, was born in New York City on the Upper West Side, and my history began there with my brother, Steven, my true companion."

That conversation was spinning in my head.

Going along a narrow path, I struggled to keep up.

"I told you some things about me the first time I wrote to you in Ann Arbor," I said.

"I remember everything you said, even the sequence. And then you turned out not to be the convent girl you promised."

I snapped a purple wildflower and put it behind my ear. "And most of what you had to say was song," I said.

"Nothing else to add," he said.

The woods opened along an old stone wall, partially destroyed, the deep crevices thick with wildflowers and moss.

"This land was private, maybe in the nineteenth century, and the owners had gardens and stone walls and fountains." He dropped back to walk along beside me. "We'll come to the place where the creek surfaces and makes an amazing racket as the shallow water goes over the rocks."

"How do you know about this place?" I asked.

"I found it once walking from Dumbarton Oaks."

"With another girl?"

"With a dog," he said.

I laughed, relieved.

"We used to live near here after my mother died, and once when I was walking my golden retriever at Dumbarton Oaks, he led me down this path, and I've never seen anyone else on it, except the homeless who've made a place for themselves near here."

"Why here?" I asked.

"They've made themselves a home," he said. "It's out of the way, and they must have discovered it like I did."

I followed him up a steep hill, the trees crowding us off the path, and I grabbed the waistband of his shorts to keep my balance.

I was in a space capsule, out of gravity's reach, and in this place, the air soft on my skin, the sun warming the top of my head, there was no room for reflection or analysis, only this moment in a new geography far from earth.

"I'm an only child, and my mother was a concert pianist from Argentina who was killed in an automobile accident when I was six," Benjamin was saying. "You know about my father."

"Only what it said in the paper."

"He and I lived together, and we had a dog, which he got so I'd have a sibling, and when one dog died, we got another. I went to school, first to the local elementary school, then to Catholic high school. The usual," he said, pulling me up a muddy bank. "I had started to make up little songs on the piano before my mother died, and then I took piano lessons and played lacrosse and did okay in school and had an ordinary, satisfactory daily life, doing the usual things a boy at a strict academic parochial school will do."

"Did you have girlfriends?"

"Not in high school, but I used to pretend I had a girlfriend who was also a composer. We wrote duets."

We had to climb up rocks, slippery with moss, to a higher plateau, not exactly a field but a break in the trees, an open space with wildflowers, the silence of early morning. I could hear the creek slipping over the rocks.

"Now you!" he said.

"You didn't answer my question."

"I've had girlfriends," he said, "but I don't have one now."

"I've had no one," I said.

It was the one true thing I told him and he laughed in disbelief.

"I didn't expect anything of that letter I sent you," I said. "Maybe sympathy about my brother, but that's all." My face was hot and damp.

"No?" Benjamin said. "You should reread your first letter. It was a love letter, as I remember."

I slid down a rock, catching him by the arm.

"I'm looking for a particular place I've always found when I walked here, and I hope I can find it now." He pulled me up a hill behind him. "It's near here, behind an old fountain that still has water coming through the mouth of a cherub, but the creek may be too dry this time of year."

I stopped, listening. I thought I heard the sound of water dripping.

"We need to make a plan," Benjamin said, leaning against a stone wall, wiping perspiration off his forehead with the back of his hand.

"What kind of plan?"

"I want to see you as much as I can before I leave the country," he said. "I've found a place to go about an hour and a half away, in the Blue Ridge Mountains," he was saying, both of us breathless from climbing. "If you tell your parents that we're going away together tonight, will they let you come with me?"

"I'm too old to have to ask them," I said, my head spinning.

"You said your family was strict."

"And Catholic, I know." I had no intention of going over the series of lies I'd told him. "But I'm out of college."

"Then it'll be easy," he said, taking off up the hill again. "As long as you want to come."

We came upon the place all of a sudden, a soft, damp blanket of grass between the fountain and the creek.

"Is this it?" I asked.

"It is," he said. "Now look over there."

Beyond us and below, no more than twenty yards, was a cup in the woods, a stretch of grass where a community of tattered souls was living under sheets drawn between the branches of trees, blankets spread on the ground, breakfast cooking in a big pot on an open fire, a village of homeless people already stirring, about their day.

"Is it safe to be so close to them?" I asked.

"Here is safe," he said.

"I mean from danger?"

"From company, Sophia."

2

I lay on my back at the edge of the Rappahannock River, the sun coming up through the mist, my hand skimming the surface of the water, Benjamin's head on my belly.

In the near distance the sound of frogs.

"Did you ever collect tadpoles?" I asked.

"Every spring from Rock Creek in a mayonnaise jar. They always died," he said, "and so I know nothing about frogs."

"*Rana temporaria*. That's their official name," I said sleepily. "Do you know how they mate?"

"I never gave it a second thought."

"You need to know." I giggled. "The male grabs the female and stimulates her to release eggs and the eggs are fertilized in the water. Very efficient and cold-blooded."

He ran his tongue across my cheek and over my nose. "I don't even like frogs," he said.

"Nevertheless, I'll tell you what you missed about frogs," I went on. "The tadpole is born with internal gills and a fish tail and during metamorphosis the gills and tail are reabsorbed and the tadpole develops walking legs."

"I thought you were a musician," he said, moving his body so his head was resting next to mine.

"I used to be a student of biology," I said.

It was the closest I came to telling Benjamin the truth.

"And your tadpoles turned into frogs?" he asked.

"They died." I said.

We had been in Virginia for two days, near the town of Orange, where the Blue Ridge Mountains faded smoky blue in the distance and the land unfolded in green hills with long vistas. We were staying in a cabin beside the river, eating at the inn, hardly eating, ordering for one, the plate between us, feeding each other dessert with our hands.

I ran my fingers through Benjamin's hair, and his eyelids fluttered open. He was beautiful, perfectly shaped, with a broad forehead, rich brown skin the color of milky coffee, his hair peppered with gray. In particular I loved his eyes, green eyes flecked with yellow, capturing the light.

"Gray at twenty-eight?" I asked.

He turned over, kissing my lips.

"Aging prematurely," he said, his breath in my mouth, our eyes wide open. "Old enough to take care of a child like you."

We had been together all day, from the first light creeping up from the bottom of the world to night, when we lay naked in the half circle of light from the crescent moon coming through the window of our ancient rickety bedroom.

We were staying in one of several small houses built after the Civil War on a large property along the river, restored to replicate the simplicity of life in the late nineteenth century. The bed was a rope bed, with a thin mattress and a light quilt, and we could hear the river running over the rocks while we lay wrapped around each other, drifting into sleep.

Before I left home, I had told my parents that they would meet Benjamin if things materialized between us.

My father said under no circumstances could I go off with someone he hadn't met.

"He *has* to say that because he's your father," Julia said as I stood in the kitchen with my backpack. But she seemed relieved for me to leave, and I imagine that she was weary—they were both weary—and didn't want to feel responsible for me any longer.

Milo was beside himself with joy.

"Will you marry him?" he asked me.

"She won't," Bernard said. "She won't be able to marry him, Uncle Milo, because we don't even know who he is."

"We know, we know," Milo said impatiently. "We listened to the music he wrote to her. So you'll marry him, won't you, Claire, and then the house will be full of music."

"Maybe. Sometime," I added, already captured in a net of my own lies. One more hardly seemed to matter.

Before I left to meet Benjamin, I checked my phone. There were six messages from Victor, calling and calling to find out what I knew.

My body against the sheets was a long silk robe. It could float without sinking on the surface of the rushing river if Benjamin were to lift me from the bed and put me in the water.

"Can you come to Prague to visit, Sophia?" he asked the night before we left Virginia, lying on the sheets, our hands barely touching. "Maybe for Christmas and New Year's."

"Maybe," I said.

"We have only begun, and a year is too long to be apart."

"I'll try to come, but it will be our first Christmas without my brother."

"Come later, then. Come for the winter or the spring or the summer. We'll take a tiny apartment above the river."

He lifted his body over mine, stretched my arms above my head, his hands in mine, our feet entwined. We were exactly the same size.

3

The morning of the day Benjamin left for Prague was hot, with a steady light rain and no wind. We drove back to Washington with the windows down, sprayed with warm rain, talking about names.

"I was named for my grandmother Sophia, who was dead when I was born," I said.

"Like me. I was named for my dead grandfather, Benjamin and my mother's father, Asa."

"So you carry on names in your family?" I asked.

"Especially in my mother's family," he said.

"We do, too."

"What about Alberto?"

"My brother was the only Alberto that I know of. I've never asked why he was given that name."

I kept straight the facts of my deception by using the details of my mother's transplanted Chilean family.

Gradually over the last days, "Sophia" had become familiar, more than familiar. My name, with the sound of sensual music drawing out the syllables—So-phi-a. The woman I had been to Benjamin for these blissful days, and who I wished I could be. I wanted to walk out of my life into this one we had made together in an isolated outpost of our common imagination.

"Would you name a boy Alberto if you had one?" Benjamin asked.

We had talked about Alberto, about his death from encephalitis, how it had been so swift, almost like an accident for the shock it had given my family.

"I don't know what I'd name a boy."

I had never considered naming, never had a reason to think of it, expecting one day to have a child.

"My brother was the only Alberto to me." I slipped out of my sandals, putting my feet against the dashboard. "I think I'd name a boy Steven."

"Steven." Benjamin pulled into a gas station north of Culpeper. "Why Steven?"

"I love the name," I said.

"An Anglo name." He patted my thigh. "It would go well with Reed, don't you think?"

I smiled. "I'd name a girl Gabriela," I said. "That's not Anglo."

"I like Gabriela."

"Or Laela. I have more girls' names that I like than boys'."

He was getting out of the car to fill up the gas tank and grabbed my hair, kissing the curly ends.

"Don't bolt while I go into the store," he said.

"I'm here forever," I replied.

I slept while he was gone, the sweet and heavy sleep of long days together, and must have dreamed, since he told me I was whimpering when he returned with a cold bottle of lemonade, touching it to my bare legs, waking me with a start.

I rolled the bottle across my damp, hot face.

"We were talking about names, remember?"

"I remember," I said.

"I would call a boy Asa."

"Did you ever meet the Asa grandfather?"

"He was my favorite person growing up." He reached down and took my hand.

"What about a girl's name?" I asked.

"Beatriz. That was my mother."

"Very beautiful."

"She was very beautiful."

"We'll need a lot of children for these names," I said.

"How many do we have?"

"Steven and Beatriz and Gabriela and Asa and Laela. Do you think we can afford five children on a composer's salary?"

"We'll manage. Five is a good number. Big enough to last."

"That's what my mother always says. A small family is no good. You need a tribe."

At a stoplight in Warrenton, he put his palm against my cheek.

"You could be pregnant, of course."

"Of course."

He laughed. "And then what?"

"Then I call you and come to Prague and we have our baby and live together in the apartment over the river."

"And marry?"

"Of course marry."

"Are you religious?" he asked.

"You mean Catholic?" I asked. "We are Catholic, raised Catholic, but I'm nothing now."

"So we'll be married by a justice of the peace or whatever equivalent they have in the Czech Republic."

We turned onto Route 66.

"Do you want lunch?"

"No lunch," I said.

We had eaten very little in the last three days, but I wasn't at all hungry.

He dropped his hand onto my bare leg, and I held it there.

"Could you be pregnant?"

"I wish," I said. "But no."

Which wasn't exactly true. In the days and nights we'd spent to-gether, I'd used no common sense. This love affair was destined to be brief and end, something Benjamin did not know and I didn't think about. I had not been careful with him. I hadn't been careful with my life for months, not since I met Victor Duarte.

"What's going to happen between us now?" he asked as we drove into town.

"We'll write back and forth, but in English, not music, this time."

We drove across the Fourteenth Street Bridge from Virginia into the city, heading to Dupont Circle, and once we were in town, nei-ther of us spoke. He pulled the car over to the curb at Dupont Circle, where we had planned to say good-bye. That evening he was due to leave for Prague.

On the grass around the circle, police stood watching the traffic, fifteen of them at least.

"No stopping there!" one of them shouted at Benjamin across the traffic.

"I'm letting someone off!" he called back.

"You can meet my parents later," I said. "When you get back next year."

"And you'll come to visit?"

"I will," I said.

But back in town, in the hustle of traffic and horns and police and the sounds of a nervous city, the cold chill of reality crawled up my spine.

"I'm sure your parents would want you to have this kind of happiness."

"I just can't promise Christmas," I said.

He dropped his hand on top of mine.

A storm of sobs was gathering in my throat, and I couldn't speak.

In retrospect, this was the moment I could have made a decision to tell Benjamin the truth, and I don't know why I didn't. Was my mind too foggy to follow the long paths of eventualities? Would I leave with him for Prague? Would Victor harm him if I told the truth? Harm me? Harm my parents?

And who was I? This person who had been with Benjamin—was this person Claire Frayn? Or the one I'd been just last month, Sophia Lupe, planning vengeance with Victor Duarte in subterranean rooms?

But there is no answer to be found in this kind of thinking.

I did what I did.

"Leave quickly, quickly," I whispered. "I don't want to see you go."

I opened the car door.

"Good-bye, good-bye, good-bye."

I kissed his cheek and shut the door.

He pulled into the traffic, entered the outside lane of the circle, and I watched his car round Connecticut Avenue, turn south on Massachusetts and disappear.

He didn't turn his head to look back at me or wave.

At the CVS drugstore, I slipped into a space between the store and movie theater, leaning against the wall. I don't cry easily, hadn't cried in the days and weeks and months since Steven's unbearable death, afraid if I gave in to tears, the weeping would never stop.

People walked by, taking me into account, hesitating, moving on, not wishing to intercede, except for a young boy pulling against his mother's hand when she urged him on.

"Are you dying?" he asked me.

I shook my head, wiping my face with my arms.

"Is she?" He turned to his mother, still holding her hand although he had moved as close to me as he could without letting go of her.

"This is not our business, Timothy," his mother said.

And she dragged the boy past me, past the movie theater, the CVS drugstore, his head still turned in my direction.

———————

On the edge of Dupont Circle, I checked my voice mail. One message from Victor.

"No luck? We'll meet tonight at Café Rouge around 9 P.M. and regroup. I called his father's house and was told Benjamin had left the country."

I moved away from the traffic noise and dialed Victor's cell.

"Benjamin had no interest in seeing me, so I never saw him," I said. "And I can't come to the Café Rouge. I can't see you. Something has come up."

I turned the cell phone off and tossed it into the trash can next to the CVS drugstore. When I got home, I would cancel my phone service and, tomorrow, the post-office box.

From Dupont Circle I walked toward Bethesda, taking the back streets, my pack heavy in the heat, my legs liquid. The rain, more mist than water, had the vague sick smell of mulberries.

It was a long walk, just under seven miles, and on the way I stopped for water, for coffee, to wander through the books at Politics and Prose, at a toy store where I bought a set of jacks, a game Steven and I used to play. He always beat me, did not even *try* to lose.

Walking north and in no hurry to get home, I left the day behind, heading toward dusk. By the time I reached our subdivision in Bethesda, the sun had almost set, orange in the west behind me. In the direction of our house, the leftover light striped the horizon, so I was walking into shadows. I had the sense of walking with the essence of Benjamin, as if the remembered chemistry of a person could take on his actual presence.

Mr. Denver was in his yard and motioned to me.

"I have tomatoes from my garden for your family," he said, handing me a plastic bag with a few ripe tomatoes in it. He smiled. Close up and under the streetlight, I could see his crooked smile and bad teeth.

"Thank you," I said. "We love tomatoes, and this year we don't have a garden."

We *never* had a garden, because the airplane hangar took up all the space in the backyard, and Mr. Denver probably knew that, but I was feeling generous that afternoon, even toward Mr. Denver.

The lights in the front of our house were off, and also those in the hangar—the kitchen light beamed a triangle across the yard as I walked down the street.

But the cars were in the driveway, so my family must be home.

I went up the front steps to the unlit porch, reached into my pack to feel around for the house key, which was at the bottom.

Standing in the steel-gray dusk, my head down, searching for the key, I had a sudden sense of presence in the darkness just beyond the porch, screened with lilac bushes and hydrangeas.

I turned, staring into the large blue hydrangea at the front, and in the bushes a form began to materialize.

"Hello? Is anybody there?"

"Sophia!"

Victor stepped out into the circle of distant light from the street-lamp, wearing Steven's old khakis cut off at the ankle and his yellow sport shirt with the tail out.

"I got your message on the voice mail," he said. "I knew where you lived."

I didn't move.

"Steven used to invite me for dinner sometimes, but I never came until now. Too much a city rat for this neighborhood."

"You got my message?" I asked. "It didn't work."

"So you said."

He moved closer to the porch.

"Did you know when you gave me these clothes that Steven had left a ten-dollar bill with my phone number on the corner of it in the pocket of the pants?"

He put the ten-dollar bill on the porch railing.

"I told you that something has come up." My voice had the thin whine of a cheap string instrument. "I can't see you, so please leave and don't come back."

I turned the key in the door and pushed it open with my shoulder. Once inside the house, I double-locked the front door, turned on the porch light to see if Victor had come out of the bushes onto the porch, but he had disappeared, melted into the night, an apparition of my imagination.

Then, in darkness, I walked through the unlit house toward the sound of laughter coming from the kitchen.

4

I lay on my back on the unmade bed in my own room, my hand on my belly, rising just above the pelvic bones like a half moon, hard to the touch.

Through the large window with which my father had replaced the south-facing wall, a gray November morning lay flat against the glass. It was almost noon, and I was late for classes.

The night in August when Benjamin left for Prague and Victor met me in the dark on the porch, I moved back into my own room from Steven's. The next morning I opened the doors and windows, dragged the furniture into the garden and scrubbed the floors and walls and windows, washed the linen, tore the dead plants out of the planter, took the boxes of my old life into the basement, where we stored the past on shelves my father had built along the wall above the washing machine and dryer.

I filled the windows with yellow hibiscus.

At night I'd lie in bed and read about human anatomy in preparation for my classes in the fall.

———————

Julia called to ask if I'd be taking the car to school, and I replied I would. Weeks ago she might have stormed into my bedroom with questions about the sudden changes in my life, but not today, although I knew she was brimming with them.

I was dressed, had already been out for breakfast with Eva and a doctor's appointment and to pick up another copy of the anatomy text, because I'd lost my copy someplace at school.

I'd been losing everything in the last few weeks—coats and books and money, my wallet, the keys to the house—distracted and sleepy all day, falling into bed right after dinner as if I had to make up for all the sleep I'd lost since Steven had died.

Julia had taken off for the day and was in the kitchen, cooking dinner for Faith's birthday that night. Bernard was probably with her, his second week at home recovering from what he called "late-onset chickenpox."

Soon I'd have to get up, brush my hair, gather my books and stop in the kitchen to talk. Julia had insisted I eat, which required conversation.

It would begin with Bernard asking me whatever had happened to the boyfriend who sent me all those songs, which was the major reason I didn't want to go to the kitchen—that and Julia's inquisition.

"We broke up," I'd say to Bernard.

Then he'd ask why we broke up, and I'd say it didn't work out, and he'd ask how come not. We could go on like that for quite a long time, since my patience had lengthened and I was no longer in a bad temper with Bernard.

"I am who I am who I am who I am," Bernard would say.

I'd broken up with Benjamin although the word "broken" doesn't at all describe the way I felt toward him, which was glued to every moment we had been together. The morning after he left for Prague,

I wrote him a short letter and then canceled my post-office box in Foggy Bottom. There was no way that he could find me. He didn't know my name, or the names of my family, where I lived. He didn't know my real life—except at the heart of it he knew everything.

Victor was another story. He knew exactly where to find me, but so far I had not heard from him, and although I went to the library at George Washington as usual, I worked in a different room. Nevertheless it would be easy to track me down, at home, at school, on the streets of Bethesda or Georgetown or Foggy Bottom.

There was nothing to do about Victor but hold my breath.

I knew by heart the letter I had sent to Benjamin, which I'd addressed to him at his father's house 310 A Street SE, Washington, D.C., expecting that it had been forwarded to Prague by late August. Two and a half months had gone by. Perhaps by now he had a Czech girlfriend and I had slipped into a shadow from his past. Or maybe he was somewhere in Prague listening to music in an old church and thinking of me as I was thinking of him.

Dear Benjamin,

This letter is linear and moves along according to the importance of what is getting said, with the most important coming first.

You are the only man I have ever loved, and I love you to distraction and beyond reason.

But I am not Sophia Lupe, not a musician, not part of a conservative Catholic family with a brother who died this year of encephalitis. Those things I made up, and my reason for this deception is the same reason I cannot see you again.

Before I ever met you, I agreed to do something terrible against you, which is why you cannot know my real name or with whom I had this plan.

My post-office box has been canceled and so has my cell-phone service. There is no way for you to get in touch with me.
Beyond sadness.

I got up, dizzy at first, and brushed my hair, moving the boxes from my old natural-history museum, which I'd packed away in the closet the day after Steven died, from the top of the bureau to his bed, where I planned to look at them before I moved, in case I wanted to bring the pallid bat or the caterpillar on blue silk to my new apartment on Capitol Hill. The kitten floating in formaldehyde, who used to be my favorite, had lost her appeal.

The apartment on Eleventh Street, southeast of the Capitol, had a bedroom and a tiny room that could be an office or a nursery. It was on the top floor of a small building near Lincoln Park and not terribly far away from the house on A Street where Benjamin's father lived.

"If you have to move, why don't you move near the university?" Julia had asked on Saturday when I found the apartment.

I had looked in Foggy Bottom, but it didn't interest me. It was too close to the place where Steven had died. On Capitol Hill it was possible that I would meet up with Benjamin's father on a long walk. Perhaps in time we would get to know each other, and he would tell me about Benjamin, the way parents do, just as a matter of conversation. Besides, Capitol Hill felt like home to me because it was where Benjamin had grown up.

I picked up my satchel of books for school and went into the kitchen.

"Julia made minestrone, and I'll get you some."

Bernard started to get up. He still had a sprinkling of pox, crusty on his cheeks, his eyes puffy. He looked quite terrible.

"What are you doing for furniture, Claire?" Julia asked, her back to me, melting chocolate for Faith's birthday cake in the double boiler. "Borrowing from home?"

"I don't need much furniture," I said.

"Take your whole room," she said. "Take Steven's room."

"I'm not going to take your furniture, Julia," I said quietly, understanding that she was hurt at my leaving and that fighting was her defense.

"Think nothing of it," she said to me. "I don't have any interest in my furniture."

"You can get some from the Salvation Army," Bernard said. "My friend Joey got a blue couch from the Salvation Army, and I've sat on it."

Julia licked the wooden spoon she was using to stir the chocolate. "You'll need help," she said. "I suppose you've thought of that already. And money. Do you have enough to pay your rent?"

"I get enough as a teaching assistant, and help I'll figure out in May."

It occurred to me watching Julia's back that she was crying. Bernard must have noticed, too. He got up from the end of the table and sat down on the chair next to me.

"Aunt Julia will help, won't she, Claire?" he said. "When you need help, she'll come to your new apartment."

"Yes, she will," I said, grateful that Bernard understood my mother's sadness, which I couldn't accommodate, not then, perhaps not ever. Sadness has the weight of nothing else I know.

Bernard had pulled his chair back and was looking at me, looking specifically at my stomach, a quizzical expression on his face.

"Can I touch it?" he asked.

"You can touch it, but you won't be able to feel anything yet," I said.

He reached over and put his blunt, squarish hand on my belly.

"See?" I said.

"It's very small now, isn't it? But I feel it. I think I feel it."

"Don't be crazy, Bernard," Julia said, turning away from the stove, her eyes bright as they always were, her face set. "What's there is no bigger than a goldfish. Inside Claire's stomach is Claire, and I hope it's a strong enough stomach to survive the crime center of Washington on Capitol Hill."

"There're lots of police around the Capitol," I said, smiling in spite of myself, glad to hear the rough edges of my mother's temperament resurfacing.

"Police! What good is that?" she asked.

"I can be Claire's bodyguard," Bernard said. "I don't like my job at the 7-Eleven. That's a serious offer."

"I know that, Bern."

I grabbed my bag and coat, kissed Julia on the cheek, and headed out the back door to Steven's car, thinking of the little goldfish doing double flips in my belly.

IX.

THE AFTERNOON OF OCTOBER 22

Dawn and my mother and I are on our way to the Eastern Market to be there when it opens at six. Julia's arm is laced through mine, our bodies touching in an awkward syncopation, our heads together. We're chattering back and forth. Such a funny pair we must seem to people on the street. A tall, skinny woman and a small, squat one walking in lockstep. No one would suspect we are related, but I have become my mother's daughter in ways I never imagined possible.

Last night at sunset, we scattered Steven's ashes offshore in the Atlantic Ocean, near the town of Lewes, Delaware, where my father had bought the lifeguard chair that we keep in our backyard.

It was Julia's sentimental idea that we go to the Atlantic Ocean, close enough to shore that bits of his ashes could wash up on the beach.

My father rented a van so we would all fit, the six of us plus Asa and Lisha. We hired a fishing boat that took us about half a mile offshore. On a clear, cold night with a perfectly shaped crescent moon, the water smooth as glass on the surface.

My father wanted a Quaker meeting with champagne, and so we sat in silence on the deck of the fishing boat as the sun went down, weeping and drinking champagne from the treble-clef glasses Julia had made in memory of Steven.

No one could find sufficient words to speak.

"Steven wasn't there," Julia said when we got into the van to go home. "That's why we couldn't talk about him."

"You expected Steven?" Milo asked.

"You never know," Julia said, reaching out to take my father's hand.

We are on our way to the market to buy food for a dinner that Julia is making today at my parents' house in Bethesda. She arrived at my apartment with a menu of lamb and couscous and ratatouille and olives and cheese and wines and plum tart, which she is making because it was Steven's favorite dessert and this dinner is in honor of his life.

Lisha will be coming, and perhaps Benjamin and his father, and our family, including Faith and Bernard and Milo.

We never had a chance to celebrate Steven's birthday in August. The food I got for lunch that day remained in the fridge for a roller-coaster month while our lives twisted and turned, settling finally to a silent, fixed point the way a car will do after a crash.

When my family arrived for lunch on Steven's birthday, I was still sitting in the chair with Asa, who had fallen asleep. Outside, I imagined Victor Duarte, leaning against a lamppost or checking the names on the apartment doorbells, waiting for me to appear.

I told my family the story of what had happened just as you have heard it, from the stormy morning of the day that Steven died to the last time I saw Victor. Julia was saying, "I know, I know," and after so much talking, I'd lost the voice to contradict her. But I was sure she hadn't known this story, had been too much on the offensive to listen, and she was stunned. Only my father had had a sense that I was in some kind of trouble.

When I finished talking, Faith, sitting on the arm of my chair, reached down and took my wrist.

"What a long, long wait to tell us, Claire," she said.

By three o'clock in the morning of the next day, the FBI had gone to Victor's basement apartment on Thirteenth Street, where by luck he still lived, with the intention of asking him some questions related to Steven's death.

They didn't need to wait. Before they had a chance to ask their questions, Victor confessed to assassinating Steven with a Beretta nine-millimeter, hiding in a basement room in Phillips Hall and shooting through a window.

Agent Burns told us what had happened later and promised that, if we wished, it would eventually be possible for us to hear the tape of Victor's confession.

I wrote to Benjamin in August to tell him the truth. We had not been in touch since the afternoon he left for Prague a year ago, and now he was back in Michigan completing his studies. He didn't write back for several weeks, and when he did, it was a short note only to say he was flying home from Detroit to meet Asa.

I have seen him several times since then. We've had dinner at the tiny table in the Reeds' kitchen while Charles Reed, a quiet, elegant man, held Asa in his lap, bent over our baby cooing bird songs in his ear.

From time to time that evening, I could feel Charles Reed looking at me, taking me into account, and the sense I had from him was curiosity that I hope might carry over to his son.

Benjamin and I are like a couple in the process of a divorce, uncertain of how to negotiate one day to the next. We speak about Asa, and if we speak about ourselves at all, it is through Asa and with little hope.

"I'd like for Asa to know his father," I will say, an intentionally loaded remark.

"He *will* know his father," Benjamin replies. "We'll make a plan for that, month to month."

Just last week, on Saturday, Benjamin flew home for the weekend, and we met at a coffee shop on Independence Avenue. A hot fall afternoon, and we sat outside, the wind behind us, blowing my hair across my face.

"I'd like Asa to spend the weekend the next time I come to Washington," Benjamin said.

"The weekend is too long while I'm nursing," I replied. "Maybe just an overnight."

"How long before he can spend the weekend?" he asked.

"I don't know, Benjamin," I said, and again, as I had already said over and over, "I am so sorry for what I did."

He looked at me quietly, assessing.

"He's got your nose," he said. "Not an entirely bad nose."

We hadn't talked about what happened or how it happened or why I got so easily involved with Victor Duarte. But that afternoon I felt a weakness in the wall of Benjamin's defenses, and I told him the story of meeting Victor at Café Rouge the first time, when he had the newspaper article with Benjamin's photograph.

"I don't understand how you could believe him with no evidence," Benjamin said.

"I just did," I said. "I was desperate to believe."

Benjamin looked off into the traffic on Independence Avenue, where a blue pickup truck was stopped behind a Metro bus, honking and honking, so it was difficult to hear above the noise.

"It's not an accident that Victor Duarte chose me, is it?" he asked.

I didn't reply. I had no answer to what he had implied by asking.

He put his head under the hood of Asa's stroller, rearranged the blanket, running his finger over his baby cheek.

"I'm going to take Asa home to see his grandfather for a while, and I'll call you when I'm ready to bring him back."

"But I have to feed him."

"I saw bottles in a thermos case in the back of his stroller," he said. "He'll be fine."

I hesitated, ready to argue, but resisted, watching him cross Independence Avenue at Second Street, walk up the block with the stroller and in the distance turn right at A Street, where his house was located, two row houses in from the corner. I wanted to follow him, to knock on the front door and insist, but I couldn't do anything except walk out Independence Avenue to Eleventh Street, run up the steps to the seventh floor of my apartment building, since the elevator was slow, and sit by the phone, which I did, weeping tears of shame and betrayal and loss, words so ordinary as to be rare and true.

Hours later he called to ask me to meet him on the stoop next to my building, since he didn't want to come to my apartment. I was waiting there when he came up the street with Asa sleeping in the stroller and sat down on one of the cold steps, leaned back on his elbows and looked at me.

"What were you thinking, Claire?" he asked. "Tell me, what were you thinking when you agreed to all of this?"

I had thought and thought about it. I had planned these conversations with Benjamin, rehearsed them at night trying to fall asleep, hoping to have the opportunity to talk to him, but he had not been willing until now, and now I had lost faith in any defense I might have had for my own actions.

"I was hopeless," I began, crunching dry leaves in my hand, and then I shook my head. "I don't know what I was thinking, Benjamin. I *wasn't* thinking. I was dead."

"But you went on and on, plenty of time to change your mind. We wrote all those letters. We spent hours and hours in your made-up story, pretending this and that, lie after lie, while I fell head over heels in love with you." His face was flushed.

Reaching into the stroller, I rearranged the blanket around Asa, pulled down the sunroof to keep the light out of his eyes. There was nothing to say, I thought, drawing my knees up under my chin.

"I turned into a stranger to myself."

We are coming to the fruit stand, where we'll buy plums and bananas and blueberries and honey—my mother gripping my hand now, demanding my attention to a conversation we have already had many times since August 11th.

But Julia is like this.

"What I find mystifying," she is saying, "is how you could wait for a year, knowing this crazy man, and not tell us about him.

"I was frozen," I say, the answer I give her every time she asks.

And it is true.

She's gathering plums, two dozen in a paper bag. "So tell me everything again."

I take a deep breath. "I met Victor at the library the first day I went back to school after Steven died. He told me that he was Steven's friend, that he loved him like brother, and then he showed me the newspaper photograph of Benjamin and said he thought Benjamin knew who had killed Steven."

We had this conversation whenever we were together, Julia always beginning as if it were the first time the subject had come up.

"After Steven died, I wanted to disappear," I say, patient with her because she deserves that from me. "When Victor told me about Benjamin, he gave me a way out. For a while, a few crazy weeks, that's how it felt."

"Enough to fall in love with somebody?"

"I fell *in* with Victor, not in love with him."

"And when did you realize he was a monster?"

"Over time, when I started to get the songs from Benjamin and wondered how could a man who writes this music be capable of killing, and then I met the woman in the ladies' room at Café Rouge, and I started to doubt. That is the first time, really the first time, I doubted anything Victor Duarte had said to me. I was that urgent to believe him."

Julia shakes her head, moving on to the vegetables, loading her bags with zucchini and tomatoes and eggplant.

"I don't understand," she says.

We move along the rows of stalls, stopping for olives.

"You never thought he was dangerous?"

"He said he was Steven's friend," I say. "He said he loved Steven, and I *wanted* to believe him."

"They were not friends," she says. "Steven would *not* have such a person as a friend."

I pull her aside from the crowd. "Mama." My hands are on her shoulders, and she has turned her head away from me. "Listen to me. Steven trusted Victor, just like I did. They *were* friends."

Julia puts her groceries down on the end of a stall, her eyes filling. For the first time since we have had these conversations the last two months, she breaks down.

"It was my fault," she says.

I shake my head. "You took too good care of us, Mama."

"I should have taught you to take care of yourselves."

She runs the back of her hand across her face, rubbing her eyes, and then she picks up the bag of groceries and we head in the direction of the butcher's to buy lamb.

The second major story about Steven's assassination was on the front page of the *Washington Post* on August 13, with a photograph of Steven taken at GWU the year he died and another photograph of Victor standing with Agent Burns and an agent I didn't know.

> At 4 a.m., August 12, the FBI arrested Victor Duarte for the murder of GWU law student Steven Frayn. Mr. Frayn was killed April 4, a year ago, on the steps of the library at George Washington University. Mr. Duarte is an unemployed and homeless engineer with a history of mental illness. The arrest was made following Duarte's confession to the police, in which he described hiding in a basement room in the building next door to the library and firing at Frayn with a 9-mm Beretta through a window when Frayn came out of the library. Victor Duarte and Steven Frayn had been acquaintances for the past year, meeting regularly at a café near George Washington University campus and sharing, according to Mr. Duarte, many of the same political views.

My mother doesn't mention Victor's taped confession until we are in the car, driving home with the dinner for Steven's celebration.

I am sitting in the back with Asa, and we're waiting for the light to change so we can turn onto Rock Creek Parkway.

"Do you think Benjamin's going to come this morning to hear the tape?" she asks.

"He says he will. He's coming with his father."

"I like his father," Julia says.

"I like him, too, but he's formal."

"Formal is good."

"Yes, formal is good, but he's too formal."

We are on the brink of a different conversation, retreating from what is about to happen this morning in our kitchen with Agent Burns from the FBI.

When we were told that the tape could be released for our hearing, that Agent Burns would bring it over to our house only if we wanted to hear it, with the clear understanding that we might be upset by it, Julia decided to make an occasion.

"Closure," she said.

"I dislike that word, 'closure,'" my father said. "It makes me sick."

I stayed out of the conversation. I didn't want to hear Victor's voice again.

"I don't know another word. All I know is that I want a ceremony to put an end to this horror in our lives. Close the door on it. Is that better?"

My father decided that if we had to listen to the tape on the day of Steven's celebration, then Benjamin and his father should be asked to come.

I understood why he wanted Benjamin at our house. In his silent way, he was angry that Benjamin came back weekends from Ann Arbor to see Asa but made no mention of a life with me.

In his own house, my father would be in charge.

"Do we have to ask Benjamin?" I asked.

Just the thought of Benjamin in our kitchen quickened my pulse.

"We've had enough trouble between us," I told Julia. "He doesn't need any more bad news about me."

"Benjamin was also a victim of Victor Duarte, and so indirectly was his father."

My father was pacing as he sometimes did when words got stuck in his throat, back and forth across the kitchen, his hands in his pockets.

"Perhaps if we're all in the same room listening to this vile man's confession, something will happen among us."

"Like what?" Julia asked. "That's just too Welsh, David, expecting a little magic to come of this horror."

"You're always saying our family is too small, Julia," my father said, resting against the sink. "If Benjamin and his father are here, and us and Bernard and Faith and Milo, we'll be sufficient to whatever Victor Duarte has to say."

I understood that my father wanted to capture all of us in a common moment of sadness or horror or relief—whatever the sound of Victor's voice brought into the room. He hoped to set in place his daughter's future, to secure my happiness, and it was daring, especially of my father, to go so far out on this long emotional limb.

"Claire," Julia begins from the front seat, taking a left on Massachusetts Avenue at the mosque, "I don't like that Benjamin won't forgive you. It's petty."

"I wouldn't want to be with someone who did what I did," I say. "What's to trust?"

"You were crazy."

"Crazy is no excuse."

"It's a forgivable condition, and you can tell him you've turned into a different person, the person that you used to be."

"He doesn't know the person that I used to be."

When Agent Burns arrives with the tape of Victor's confession, I'm slicing white and purple eggplants, cooking them in onions and garlic on the top of the stove, with Bernard standing too close. I tell myself that Bernard is a puppy and needs to rub up against us to feel connected.

Julia is making plum tarts.

"It's the wrong honey," Bernard says. "Steven liked clover honey. It was his favorite, and he put it on toast."

"This is very high-class honey, Bern. We only use it for important occasions," Julia says.

My father sits with his feet on a chair, trying to appear at ease, talking to Benjamin. Asa is draped over Benjamin's shoulder like a shawl, and I wish they would stay just as they are, sitting in our kitchen with the far-off autumn sun streaming across the bundle of Asa peering around the room.

I wipe my hands on the apron and make a place in the middle of the table for Agent Burns to put the tape recorder.

We pull up chairs, Faith and Bernard side by side, Milo next to me, Julia on the other side, Benjamin between my father and me at the other end of the table.

Agent Burns puts his chair next to Benjamin, sits down, and, reaching to the middle of the table, he pushes "play."

"So here goes. Brace yourselves," Agent Burns says. "The other voice you hear besides Mr. Duarte's is mine."

AGENT BURNS: Identify yourself.

VICTOR DUARTE: I call myself Victor Duarte.

BURNS: Is that the name on your birth certificate?

DUARTE: The name on my birth certificate is Donny Frazier.

BURNS: Why did you change your name?

DUARTE: I'd been looking for a new name. A man called Victor Duarte died on March 6 a few years ago, and I read his name in the obituaries in the *Washington Post* and decided to take it.

BURNS: Why did you want a new name?

DUARTE: Donny Frazier had bad associations for me.

BURNS: What kinds of associations?

DUARTE: They are personal.

BURNS: How old are you?

DUARTE: Twenty-eight years old. Twenty-nine tomorrow.

BURNS: Where were you born?

DUARTE: Washington, District of Columbia.

BURNS: Do you know the name Steven Frayn?

DUARTE: He was my friend.

BURNS: You said you were the one who killed him, is that correct?

DUARTE: That is correct.

BURNS: Where did you meet Mr. Frayn?

DUARTE: I saw his photograph in the newspaper and tracked him down.

BURNS: Why would you want to track him down?

DUARTE: Because I needed to find out if he was related to Dr. David Frayn, who was going to be my father when I was ten years old and then he backed out.

There was a cracking in the tape—someone, perhaps Agent Burns coughed, stopped the tape—and when it started again, Victor was speaking. I was unable to look at my father except to note that Julia was pressed against him, lending the force of her body to his.

DUARTE: My mother had a neurological disease, and she was atrophying internally—like dried prunes, is what a nurse told me—and she got accepted at the National Institutes of Health as a research patient, and Dr. David Frayn was her doctor.

BURNS: What happened to her?

DUARTE: She died.

BURNS: What were the circumstances of her death?

DUARTE: Dr. David Frayn couldn't save her. Those were the circumstances.

BURNS: She was expected to die, is that true?

DUARTE: That is true. I asked her before she died if I could be adopted by Dr. David Frayn, and she said she would ask him, but she died before she had an opportunity, so I had to ask him myself.

BURNS: What did Dr. Frayn say when you asked him?

DUARTE: He said he couldn't adopt me because I already had relatives downtown who would adopt me.

BURNS: Was he correct?

DUARTE: He was correct, but that's not why he didn't adopt me. He didn't adopt me because he already had one son, whose name was Steven Frayn, and that was that.

Benjamin, who is in my line of sight, hands Asa to my father, pushes his chair back from the table, tips it against the wall and closes his eyes.

BURNS: What happened to you after your mother died?

DUARTE: I moved in with my mother's sister and her husband, who lived first in Pennsylvania and then on Capitol Hill, and I went to elementary school there and then to high school and then two years in engineering at the University of Maryland, and then my aunt and uncle moved to Cincinnati, so I was homeless, and I started to think about Dr. David Frayn again.

BURNS: Did you try to contact him?

DUARTE: I knew where he lived, and I knew his telephone number and that he worked at George Washington University Hospital and taught in the medical school there, so I started to go to the Gelman Library hoping to see him, and sometimes I'd drive by the Frayns' house in Bethesda or call them from a public telephone and hang up.

BURNS: What did you want from the Frayns?

DUARTE: I wanted a home. A lot of people live with them. I've seen them go in and out of their front door.

BURNS: Did you ever contact Dr. Frayn?

DUARTE: I did not.

BURNS: What about Steven Frayn? Did you contact him?

DUARTE: I saw a photograph of Steven Frayn in the *Washington Post* two years ago, and he was at a vigil for a hate crime against a GWU student who was homosexual. That's when I called Steven Frayn at his house in Bethesda.

BURNS: What did you say to him?

DUARTE: I told him I'd read about him in the newspaper, that I admired what he'd done, that I'd looked him up on the Internet and found out he'd written a lot of articles and op-ed pieces, so I told him I agreed with his politics and would like to meet him.

BURNS: Did you meet?

DUARTE: We met at the Café Rouge every Tuesday for a beer and then every Thursday, too, and pretty soon we were meeting or talking on the telephone every day. We were friends. He thought I was a member of DTT and a revolutionary, and he thought I was very smart. I'm the one who told him I was a member of DTT and a revolutionary and very smart.

BURNS: When did you decide to kill him?

DUARTE: I decided slowly. At first I just wanted to know him, and then as I got to know him, having drinks almost every night, I wanted to have his life. He had everything—a girlfriend and a sister and a mother and aunts and uncles. And Dr. David Frayn, who had loved my mother.

BURNS: What do you mean that Dr. Frayn loved your mother?

DUARTE: He loved her. I would sit on the chair by her bed, and Dr. Frayn would come in. His hair was black then, and he had a beard, and he'd ask me to leave so he could undress her.

BURNS: He was her doctor. That's what doctors do to take care of patients, yes?

DUARTE: Yes. But he loved her, and he should have been my father.

BURNS: What made you decide on April 4 to kill Steven Frayn?

DUARTE: I had a gun. I'd had a gun for a long time and never had an occasion to use it. On April 2, Steven Frayn showed me an op-ed piece he had written for the *Washington Post* and it was full of *my* ideas, so I asked him if he would include my name on the op-ed piece, and he said no. That's when I decided to do what happened on April 4, but I'd been thinking about it for a long time.

BURNS: So you killed him because he didn't want your name to be on the op-ed piece, is that right?

DUARTE: That's not exactly right. I killed him because he took up too much room in my life.

BURNS: What made you decide to go into the basement of Phillips Hall?

DUARTE: It was a place I had spent the night before, because it's in the basement and it's full of furniture and no one ever checks it out. So we met for a beer at Café Rouge in the afternoon, and he told me he was meeting his sister, Claire, at the library at five o'clock and had to be home for dinner at seven and would I call him later. I went to the window in the basement of Phillips, which has a view of the front steps to the library, and I stayed there until I saw him with my telescopic lens, standing at the top of the steps just ahead of his sister, Claire.

BURNS: After you shot Steven Frayn, what did you do?

DUARTE: I went home.

BURNS: Where is home?

DUARTE: That night I slept in the basement of an abandoned house on Thirteenth Street, and in the morning I got up early to see if the story of Steven's death had made the front page of the *Washington Post*, which it had. That's where I live in the winter.

BURNS: Do you know Claire Frayn?

DUARTE: I do.

BURNS: Where did you meet her?

DUARTE: After Steven died, I went to the library every day, taking a seat in the main reading room at the table where Steven usually worked. One day she came in just as I expected and sat down next to me.

BURNS: What did you do?

DUARTE: I introduced myself and told her I was Steven's friend and would of course be her friend, too.

BURNS: Did you become friends?

DUARTE: Not really. She liked me, but I didn't like her. I'm not attracted to tall and skinny women. Her nose was too big, and there were other things I didn't like.

BURNS: But you saw each other.

DUARTE: We had a plan. She called it a mission.

BURNS: What plan?

DUARTE: I showed her a picture of Benjamin, which I had seen in the newspaper and cut out, and I told her that I thought Benjamin was implicated in her brother's death.

BURNS: Did you have any reason to think that was true?

DUARTE: I hated him.

BURNS: Did you have any reason to hate him?

DUARTE: He was cruel to me when I was in elementary school and ridiculed me after my mother died, and I needed to punish him.

BURNS: So you decided to tell Claire Frayn that he was responsible for her brother's death even though you had no reason at all to believe that?

DUARTE: That's true.

BURNS: And Claire went along with your story?

DUARTE: She believed me.

BURNS: Have you seen her lately?

DUARTE: I haven't seen her since Benjamin Reed came to town and she was supposed to meet up with him but he was too busy and had to go to Prague in the Czech Republic.

BURNS: When is the last time you saw her?

DUARTE: I went to the Frayns' house in August a year ago, and she was there and said she didn't want to see me again. So I left. I didn't want trouble.

BURNS: Do you have anything to add, Mr. Duarte?

DUARTE: You didn't ask me about the flag.

BURNS: Did you put the Justice Department flag on the Frayns' front porch?

DUARTE: I did.

BURNS: Did you have a reason for that?

DUARTE: I wanted them to know I was here and that I knew where they lived and I had important connections, so I was able to get a flag from the Justice Department. Especially I wanted Dr. David Frayn to know. That's all.

BURNS: Thank you, Mr. Duarte.

DUARTE: I don't call myself Victor Duarte any longer.

BURNS: What do you call yourself now?

DUARTE: I call myself Steven Frayn.

My father is sitting in his office chair, the chair tilted so far back it could easily overturn, his crossed ankles resting next to the propeller. He's facing the garden and hears me come in the door.

"Claire?"

"It's me."

"Has everyone gone?"

"Benjamin and his father have left."

"For good?"

"They're coming back for dinner," I say.

He hasn't turned around, so I'm standing behind him, hesitant, as if I expect after what he just heard in Victor Duarte's confession that his face will be changed beyond recognition.

"At least I hope Benjamin and his father are coming," I said. "That's what they said when they left."

My father stands, pulls his chair away from the plane, turns it toward me and pulls up another chair—all of this without facing me, and I am watching every gesture as if each has particular significance and will define the meaning of this day.

When he finally turns, motioning for me to take his office chair, I gasp because there's no difference in his face except the accumulated light, perhaps from the brightness of the day filtering through the Plexiglas window.

I sit down, tucking my legs under me.

"Did the Reeds have anything else to say?" he asks.

"Charles Reed said something to Faith. I couldn't hear, but he put his hand on her arm, so I suppose what he had to say was sweet."

"And Benjamin?"

"I could tell Benjamin was horrified. He couldn't even look at me." I slipped off my shoes, dropping them on the floor. "I'm not surprised about anything Victor said. Maybe nothing surprises me any longer."

"It was no one's fault, Claire."

"I know that."

He's looking out the window, straight into the noon sun. "We never know what we are in other people's lives."

"Did hearing Victor's confession make you feel better?"

"Not better. Relieved," he says. "What about you?"

"I don't excuse myself for what I did," I say, not ready to take in what I've just heard.

"We do our best," he says. "I think that's the human inclination, and if the stars reconfigure to bring such unlikely people as all of us into the same orbit, that's what happens."

I'm not exactly sure what he's saying, but he's done with this conversation, and it will suffice that I figure it out in my own time.

He wants to show me the completed airplane, and we walk around it while he points out how he fixed the wing with parts from other planes, how he reassembled the engine and put together the propeller and refurbished the interior.

"It's done," he said.

"Now what?" I ask after he finishes talking and we are heading out of the hangar toward the house.

He takes my face in his hands, kisses my forehead.

"Now life, my treasure," he says.

242

Dusk, the sun slipping down the horizon, and in the kitchen Faith and Charles are sitting on stools with glasses of wine. I can tell they are pleased to be together. But that is all. Pleased.

In my bedroom, where I go to put on a different shirt, Julia is sitting on the end of the bed, a bunch of yellow gerbera daisies on her lap.

"From the Reeds," she says of the daisies. "What did your father have to say?"

"He's finished his airplane."

I open my closet and check my blouses, deciding instead to wear a dress for Steven's celebration, a red dress made of thin wool that I got in New York on a trip we took there when I graduated from college.

"Nice choice," Julia said. "Red is good on you." She showed no evidence of leaving, so I took off my trousers and sweater, put the dress on and pulled it down over my hips.

"You've changed," she said. "You know that."

I went to the mirror above my dresser and brushed my hair, piling it loosely on top of my head.

"Do you remember when you used to call me a student of living things, before I even knew very much about biology."

"I'm a mother. I wanted to say something that I hoped would be true."

"I paid attention," I said.

She follows me out of bedroom, dropping the daisies in a vase on the kitchen table, taking the lamb out of the oven.

In the living room, where I go to tell Milo, who is practicing his concert for the celebration of Steven's life, that he is needed to carve the lamb, Julia and my father sit with a giggling Asa balanced on my father's legs, my father's face nestled in the baby's soft belly.

"Tell me, how are things now?" Julia asks.

"Things" refers to Benjamin, and I have nothing to report.

"No change," I say. "You'll be the first to know if anything happens, Mama. He's coming in the house now."

Bernard opens the door for Benjamin, who's carrying a case of wine with flowers on the top of the box, held in place with his chin. I watch him walk through the hall, into the kitchen, and for no expressed reason—he has said nothing personal to me, made no gesture in my direction, no mention of this morning's revelations—there's the scent of possibility in the air.

Milo trots into the kitchen looking for all the world like a mad musician, his hair flying, his glasses balanced precariously on the end of his nose.

"Speak to me," he says, clapping Benjamin on the back, taking the flowers off the top of the box, handing them to Bernard.

"We need a vase," he says.

Bernard looks bewildered. He reaches into a cabinet, takes out a vase and hands it to me.

"Have you recovered from this morning?" Milo asks with a shade too much cheerfulness as he puts his long fingers into kitchen mitts, opening the oven to take out the lamb.

"I'm not going to recover," Benjamin says.

"Oh, dear, I thought it would be better," Milo says. "I thought it would be much better to know Victor was insane."

I look over at Benjamin, who's watching me as he opens the case of wine, and I sense, the way a body's chemistry has its own language, that something is happening between us.

"Did Claire tell you she's becoming a composer?" Bernard asks. "I think she's very good."

"I knew she'd given it some thought," Benjamin says, taking the bottles of red wine out of the box.

"But I've decided to be a biologist, Bernard," I say. "I'm a terrible composer, but I'm hoping to be a good biologist."

At the stove Julia is making couscous.

I want to talk to Benjamin and don't know how to begin, but it seems necessary to have the conversation about Victor, so I'm thinking of how to bring up the subject without upsetting him, when he leans against the counter where I'm standing.

"What are we going to do now?" he asks quietly in my ear so no one else can hear.

"What are we going to do?" I say in response, since I have no answer except to repeat his question as reply.

We have paired off in separate places in the kitchen, waiting for Lisha to arrive before the celebration can begin. My father comes in with Asa over his shoulder, Asa's baby head stretched up out of its body shell like a turtle's. My father leans over to Julia, saying something that makes her smile. Bernard is helping with dinner, putting the lamb on a platter as Milo carves. Faith is locked in conversation with Charles Reed.

I stand beside Benjamin, tentative in the moment, as if at any second the direction of the wind could change.

"Do you want to talk about what happened today?" I ask.

"I want to play the piano," he says, moving away from the sink. "Come with me."

And I follow him to the living room, slide onto the piano bench beside him.

"Fast and witty or slow and melancholy?" he asks, his long fingers resting lightly on the keys.

I hear Lisha's car pull up to the curb, so we'll be starting soon.

"Very, very fast," I say. "We're about to begin the celebration."

The table is set with wineglasses and champagne, so we'll be very drunk by nightfall. There's an empty chair for Steven—Julia has insisted on that—and thirty white balloons filled with helium are tied to the railing on the front porch. After dinner, after the toasts and the drinking and the tears, Julia plans that we'll take the balloons outside in the garden next to the hangar, let go of the long strings, and they will illuminate the night sky with full moons.